HOLIDAY HAVEN

A CHRISTIAN MEDICAL ROMANCE

MONROE FAMILY SERIES

LAURA SCOTT

CHAPTER ONE

Adam Monroe rolled his shoulders and bent his head from side to side, working the crook out of his neck, fighting to hide the depth of his exhaustion. "Doris, this is the last patient, right?"

"Yes, I placed the infant and mother in exam number two." Doris, his receptionist, glanced at him with a frown. "You didn't eat lunch, did you?"

"No." There hadn't been time. He munched a stale cracker as he logged into the last patient's chart. They'd been extremely busy all day and well into the evening but he knew the true source of his fatigue was plain, old ordinary lack of sleep. Ever since the Christmas season had hit, the nightmares of the car accident had returned. He shook off the feeling of despondency and glanced at Doris's concerned features. "Don't worry, I'll make up for it at dinner."

"Maybe teaming up with the public health department to offer medical care to low-income families wasn't such a good idea," Doris said in a low tone. "You're exhausted."

"I'm fine." As one of the founding partners of the

private practice pediatric clinic, he was proud of their success. Tuesday evenings were reserved for the public health department referrals. The first appointment was free, and if any patients needed more extensive care and follow up, subsequent visits were prorated according to income level. Which meant basically subsequent visits were pretty much free, too. "We're providing a great service. And besides, you know I'd normally have Phoebe's help with this."

"True." Doris sighed. "I'll be glad when she's back from her second honeymoon."

Phoebe Cooper was his nurse practitioner, who usually shared his patient load, especially the infants. As she was currently off in the Caribbean, celebrating her tenth wedding anniversary, he was on his own.

His stomach growled as he walked down the hall, mentally reviewing the notes he'd seen in the chart. This patient was a two-month-old baby, and he mentally prepared himself as he knocked briefly on the door before walking in.

"Good evening, Ms. Turner," he greeted the young mother, who paced the room while holding a crying baby against her shoulder. "I'm Dr. Monroe. I understand Grady has been very fussy and has been running a low grade fever for the past twenty-four hours."

"Yes." Grady's young mother appeared extremely frazzled, as she bobbed the baby up and down, patting the infants back. The distress in her expression made him fear she might start sobbing herself. "He cries constantly. I tried feeding him, changing him, holding him—everything! Nothing works. There's something seriously wrong with him, I just know it."

"I'll take a look," Adam promised. "Excessive crying is

very frustrating and can be from something simple like an ear infection or colic." He maintained a professional demeanor, washing his hands in the sink and flashing Grady's mother a reassuring smile. He wished Phoebe was here to take this case.

"Would you please set him down on the table for a moment so I can examine him?" When she did so, he performed a thorough assessment. He tried to remain objective. When dealing with small infants, the history from the caregiver and the physical exam were the most important keys to an accurate diagnosis.

Grady's temperature was normal, his eyes and ears were clear, no sign of infection. His heart and lungs sounded good, but as abdomen was tense with hyperactive bowel sounds. He asked about the baby's eating habits and bowel movements and discovered Grady's mother was using a dairy based formula.

He handed the infant back with a sense of relief. "He's not running a fever now. I believe Grady has colic. He likely has an intolerance to milk, so I'd like you to try some soy based formula for two weeks. I'll give you some samples, so you don't have to buy any unless it helps." He washed his hands again, while Ms. Turner dressed the baby in his dark blue sleeper. "If that doesn't work, bring him back here and we will try something else. You were right to bring him in to see us. Babies shouldn't cry all the time."

"Thank you, Dr. Monroe." Her eyes filled with gratitude. Sometimes new mothers just needed a little bit of reassurance.

"I'll give you some information on colic. There are some other tricks you can try, like using a baby swing or as silly as it sounds, placing the car seat on top of your dryer while doing laundry. The motion and the sound seem to help settle a baby's upset stomach." He sat for a moment at the computer, brought up Grady's chart, and made a few notes. Then he quickly logged off. "I'll have Doris give you the formula samples, all right?"

"Yes." Grady's mother was already bundling him into his car carrier. "Thanks again for everything."

"You're welcome. Have a good evening." Adam left the exam room, and almost ran into Doris. "Oh, please take some soy formula to Grady's mother."

"Sounds good."

Back in his office he stared at the package of stale crackers, fighting a wave of grief. As a pediatrician, he knew he couldn't avoid taking care of babies. They were the mainstay of his practice. He closed his eyes and rubbed his temple. How long would the past haunt him? To be fair, it had only been a year, but the Christmas decorations surrounding him didn't help. His memories of the past just wouldn't stay buried.

Somehow he needed to find the strength to get through this Christmas holiday. At least he had a warm, loving, generous family to distract him from his guilt.

Time to finish up his documentation and get out of there. He logged back into the computer, reviewing his patients notes. Once he'd made sure everything was in order, he sent electronic copies to of each record to the public health department. Other physicians provided care, too and they needed to be kept in the loop on what was going on.

His stomach grumbled again. While he wasn't really in the mood, he knew he needed to eat. Fast food didn't appeal, but it was quick and easy and would stop the gnawing in his belly.

Maybe. Unless he had an ulcer.

"Adam!" Doris called out from the reception desk. "Come here, quick. Someone left a baby!"

What? Adam levered himself out of his seat, heading straight to the waiting area, thinking Doris had to be mistaken. "Are you sure?"

Doris waved a hand at the empty waiting room. Well, almost empty waiting room. "See for yourself. That baby wasn't there thirty minutes ago."

He stared, not sure if his glucose deprived brain was playing tricks on him. He blinked. Nope, still there. A small, crying baby, safely tucked into an infant car seat which had been left on one of the waiting room chairs.

"I'll check the bathrooms," Doris said over her shoulder as she headed down the hall to the public restrooms their office shared with an adult walk in clinic across the hall.

Adam stepped closer. The baby was dressed from head to toe in a bright pink sleeper. Unless the color was some sort of bizarre joke, he assumed the baby was a girl. He gauged her to be six-weeks-old, her tiny face scrunched and red from crying.

A folded slip of was tucked between the baby and the car seat cushion. Fearing the worst, he pulled it out and read the words, carefully printed. *I'm sorry but I can't take care of Joy anymore. I love her, but I can't afford to keep her. I brought her here because she's been running a fever for the past two days.*

Abandoned? Someone had actually left a safe haven baby in his waiting room?

"There's no sign of a parent anywhere—I even checked the men's room!" Doris planted her hands on her hips. "I can't believe this."

Adam handed her the note. "You're sure you didn't see anyone drop her off?"

"I'm positive. You know how busy we were. After putting the last patient into an exam room, I spent the rest of the time getting caught up my computer work. I didn't see or hear anyone come in." Her eyes widened when she read the note. "I can't believe it! We've never had a safe haven baby like this. Who would give up their child three weeks before Christmas?"

The baby's crying, which didn't quite sound right, grated on his nerves. He had a new appreciation for why Grady's mother had appeared so frazzled. "Pick her up, will you? Bring her back to one the exam rooms. I'll need to assess her."

Doris was already working the buckle on the car seat. The minute Doris lifted the baby against her shoulder, Joy quieted down. "Oh, my, she really is warm."

Adam grabbed the car seat. It sounded like the baby's mother was right about the child's fever. "Take her into the first exam room."

Doris carefully set the baby girl on the exam table. "Do you think she's hungry?"

"Yes. Go ahead and make a bottle from the samples of formula. We don't know when she was last fed. Sounds like the mother has been in a financial crunch." Thankfully he always carried a sizeable stockpile of extra supplies in case of emergencies.

Like this.

Doris hustled off, leaving him to carefully remove the bright pink sleeper. Doris was right—the baby radiated heat from her tiny body. When he checked her temperature, he wasn't surprised to discover her fever was high, 103.4 degrees Fahrenheit.

Joy's sound had a barking sound to it. He listened to her lungs not surprised to hear diminished breath sounds.

Could the baby have RSV—respiratory syncytial virus? He needed to do more tests, cultures and maybe an X-ray of her chest. This baby needed more care than he could provide here, in his clinic.

Even taking Joy to the hospital, though, wouldn't necessarily help him provide a firm diagnosis. He didn't have a caregiver to give him a complete history. How well was she eating? How long had she had this barking cry? How many hours did she sleep at a time? Too many questions without answers.

"I have a bottle," Doris said, entering the room. "I hope she'll take it."

He hoped so, too. There was no way of knowing if Joy's mother had breastfed her, bottle fed her, or used a special soy based formula. All he could do is hope for the best through trial and error.

Once he had finished his exam, he bundled Joy back into her pink sleeper, fumbling a bit with the snaps. He intended to hand the baby straight over to Doris, she was more of an expert in this area than he was, but the moment he lifted Joy against his chest, she quieted down.

Awestruck, he stared down at her for a long moment. She was beautiful, her dainty features perfect. Tearing his gaze from her tiny face, he forced himself to think like a doctor. Joy's weight was slightly on the low side for six-weeks-old, and reinforcing the mother likely couldn't afford to feed the child. Breast milk was free, but some women struggled to make that work.

"Do you want me to try and feed her?" Doris asked still holding the bottle.

"Yes, please." Oddly reluctant, he handed the baby over, knowing he should use this time to finish documenting the incident. He'd never had a safe haven baby left in his clinic before. Technically, safe haven babies were to be left at hospitals, police stations or fire stations.

Did a clinic count? He wasn't sure.

The baby latched onto the nipple for a few minutes, sucking eagerly. But she didn't take nearly as much nourishment as he would have liked. Too soon she let go and turned her face away.

"Now what?" Doris wrinkled her forehead and concern. "She didn't drink very much."

"I'll take her to Children's Memorial Hospital as a direct admission. Her fever needs attention." He didn't see an alternative. He couldn't do a complete work up here, his clinic wasn't equipped with a full lab or radiology services. Joy's ears had looked clear, but he wanted blood and spinal fluid cultures. "Please get the baby tucked back into the car seat."

While Doris did as he asked, he grabbed his coat. Winter in Milwaukee, Wisconsin, was cold. He searched through his cabinets to find a baby blanket, tossing it over the car seat to protect Joy's face from the frigid temperatures.

Joy began to cry again, the sound only partially muffled by the blanket. He forced himself to ignore the pathetic sound as he hefted the infant seat in one hand and headed for the door.

"Wait—don't you think we should call the police?" Doris followed him through the clinic and out to the waiting room. She looked concerned, as if she wanted to follow him all the way to the hospital. It was on the tip of his tongue to ask her to come along with him, but that was ridiculous. There was nothing Doris could do.

"I'm not sure we can, mothers of safe haven babies are not considered criminals." He hesitated, then added, "I'll check with my brother, Alec. He's a sergeant for the Milwaukee Police Department. He might have some advice. Go home, Doris. Thanks for your help."

Ducking his head against the cold December wind, his feet crunched on snow and ice as he carefully made his way to his car.

With new respect for mothers who lugged their babies around on a regular basis, he secured the infant seat in the back. It took him several tries to figure out how to get the carrier buckled in. After closing the back door, he quickly slid behind the wheel. His office wasn't far from Children's Memorial Hospital And he let the car run for a few minutes to warm up the engine.

Joy's cries echoed throughout the interior of the car. He gripped the steering wheel, unable to do anything to stop her crying. He hadn't felt this helpless since the accident last year. His son would have been almost five months old if he'd lived. "Hang in there, Joy, we're almost there." Adam glanced at the car seat in the rearview mirror but couldn't see the baby's face. Infant carriers had to be placed backwards to protect the baby from harm. He continued to talk to her, hoping the sound of his voice would help let her know she wasn't alone.

His attempts to calm her were in vain. She was still crying when he eased into traffic, using his hands free phone to call Alec.

"Hey, Alec," Adam greeted his brother when he answered the phone. "I have a small problem."

"What's up?" Alec paused and then added, "Is that a baby?"

"Yeah. That's my problem." Adam sighed. "She was left in my clinic, as a safe haven baby I assume. I'm taking her to

Children's Memorial. Would you be able to meet me there? I don't want to mess this up."

"Sure." Alec didn't hesitate. "I need to arrange for someone to watch Shannon. Jillian's at work. I don't expect her for another hour or so."

A flash of guilt nagged at him. He hated dragging his brother from his family. Alec and Jillian were doing their best to make their opposite schedules work. "Don't rush, you can wait until Jillian gets home. See you later." He disconnected the call and pulled into the parking lot of Children's Memorial Hospital.

"We're here, Joy." Unbuckling the car seat was almost as complicated as getting it put together. "Don't cry, everything's going to be fine."

Adam was relieved he could admit the baby to the hospital where he and the nursing staff could keep a close eye on her. And it would only be a matter of time before social services and the department of child protective services got involved. In a safe haven situation, there was usually not an attempt to track the mother. But in this case, because the mother made it sound like the issue was financial, he wondered if they could make an exception. The public health department had a variety of programs, as did Children's Memorial Hospital. Maybe Joy's mother didn't realize the resources that were available to her.

He wanted to reunite Joy with her mother. Unless of course her mother was unfit related to drug or alcohol abuse.

Either way, his first job was to identify the source of Joy's fever.

"ADMITTING JUST CALLED with a new patient. This one is yours, Krista."

"No problem." Krista glanced up from the computer and the chart she was reviewing. Emily, charge nurse for Six South, had taken the last admission, so indeed this new patient was hers. She didn't mind. She liked this unit, where patients were newborn infants up to the age of about two years. She was relatively new in her role, but learned something every day. "Where is the admission coming from? The emergency department?"

"Nope, Dr. Monroe is bringing this one over as a direct admission. The patient is a six-week-old baby girl with a fever of unknown origin. Put her in bed 618, as it's directly across from the nurse's station."

Krista momentarily froze. Dr. Monroe? As in Adam Monroe?

"Krista?" She glanced up to see Emily frowning at her. "Is something wrong?"

"No, of course not," she lied. Logging off the computer she stood. "I'll make sure the room is set up."

Ducking into the empty patient room, she leaned against the wall, trying to calm her racing heart. Over the past six months, since she'd started this job, she'd never had to take any of Adam's patients. She'd seen him on the unit now and then, but so far he hadn't recognized her. He'd simply nodded or said hello before going on his way.

She'd known this day would come but fell woefully unprepared for it now. Talking to him after a full year, would be awkward.

Why on earth was he bringing a direct admission in himself? She swallowed hard. Maybe he wouldn't stay long, simply drop the patient off and leave.

Pushing away from the wall, she managed to pull

herself together. She went to the supply room to fetch an LP tray, knowing that babies with fevers usually needed a lumbar puncture procedure. When she returned, she set the equipment near a small procedure table.

She sighed, forcing herself to admit that dropping the baby off wouldn't be Adam Monroe's style. He had a reputation for being extremely thorough. Everyone liked him. Nurses had been known to seek his attention.

She couldn't blame them—if circumstances were different, she might have sought his attention, too.

After making sure there were enough sterile drapes in the drawer of the procedure table, she stepped back and tucked a stray strand of hair that had fallen from the from her ponytail behind her ear. There was no reason to worry. If Adam Monroe hadn't recognized her by now, he wasn't likely to. She had grown out her badly bleached short hair and let her natural dark brown color shine through. She'd also had laser surgery for her near sightedness as her eyes hadn't been able to get accustomed to contact lenses. The laser surgery had been something of a necessity. On her second day of orientation, an eight-month-old boy had grabbed her glasses and tossed them to the floor, forcing her to wear the broken glasses for the remainder of her shift.

Regardless of why she'd slightly altered her appearance Krista knew she looked different compared to a year and a half ago, when she first met Adam. He had dated her older sister Danielle, the two of them becoming engaged after a short period of time. She hadn't seen him since last Christmas, after Danielle had broken off their engagement and moved overseas.

She'd only spoken with Adam a couple of times, having been away at college for much of the time he and Danielle had dated. Did he even remember she'd been enrolled in a nursing program? Her most vivid memory was of the night he'd picked up Danielle while her Aunt Beatrice had been there. Krista had been concerned when the woman had lost her balance, twice. She'd asked Adam to take a look and between them they'd examined Bea, quickly coming to the conclusion that she had a minor stroke.

Those moments they'd worked together had proved she'd made the right choice in becoming a nurse. A good thing, as she'd only had one more semester to go before graduating.

She crossed over to smooth the sheet over the crib mattress. She pulled out an extra blanket and set it at the foot of the crib. Glancing around, she noted everything was ready. There wasn't anything more for her to do.

Except to stand there, anticipating Adam's arrival. Hiding in her patient's room. How pathetic. Hadn't she changed at all over the past eighteen months? More so than her outward appearance, she'd been striving to become more self-confident, more outgoing and assertive.

Enough time had passed for her to get over her secret crush on Adam Monroe.

Danielle wouldn't have hidden in an empty patient room. Her older sister had always reacted a little differently to things than she had. When they'd been shuffled from one relative's house to the other, Danielle had only gotten into more trouble, while Krista had become quieter and even more well-behaved. She loved her sister, had really missed her since Danielle had moved to take a job in London.

"Which room?" She heard a deep male voice ask.

"Right behind you in 618." Emily's voice was clear. "I think Krista is in there, getting things ready."

"Thanks."

She barely had time to turn around before Adam

walked in, cradling a baby against his chest with one hand and carrying the infant carrier with the other.

For a moment their gazes locked, his mesmerizing green eyes, holding her captive. She almost took a step back from the impact. Instead, she forced herself to stand her ground.

"Krista? Krista Vaughn?" He stared at her, recognition dawning in his eyes. "How long have you worked here?"

CHAPTER TWO

"I—uh, about six months." Adam had recognized her. She couldn't believe he'd recognized her. A secret thrill warred with disappointment. Obviously, she didn't look as different as she'd hoped. She cleared her throat, willing herself not to say something stupid. She stepped aside to give him access to the crib. The sleeve of his leather coat brushed against her arm as he sent the infant seat aside then gently placed the baby on the mattress. His musky male scent, intermixed with leather, clouded her senses.

Bringing back memories she found impossible to ignore.

Focus on their patient, she told herself sternly. He stepped away just as she moved forward and they bumped into each other. His hand came up to grasp her arm, steadying her. She hoped her reaction to his touch wasn't too noticeable as she asked, "Who is this little girl you have here?"

"Joy Smith, for lack of anything better." Adam let her go and took a step back. She could still feel the warm imprint from his grasp on her arm. Her cheeks burned as she quickly busied herself with the baby.

Then his words registered. "For lack of anything better?" She frowned, unzipping the baby's sleeper. "Don't you know her name?"

"Her first name is Joy, but I don't know her last name." He tunneled his hand through his sable colored hair, leaving it mussed. "She was left in my waiting room. I'm assuming as a safe haven baby."

"You're kidding." Her initial discomfort faded. Adam had recognized her but hadn't mentioned or asked about Danielle. Did that mean he'd gotten over her sister? She sincerely hoped so as Danielle was dating somebody else. And from what she could tell, her sister's relationship was serious. Her gaze dropped back to the crying infant. A safe haven baby? She had never cared for one before. "She feels warm."

"Yes, her last rectal temp was 103.4 degrees. I need you to start an IV and draw blood cultures. Once that is finished, we'll need to do a lumbar puncture."

She picked up the baby, who immediately quieted against her. "I'll call for the procedure team, I'm sure there's a resident available to do the lumbar puncture."

He frowned, shaking his head. "No. I'll do it."

"You?" Krista couldn't hide her surprise. The hour was late, eight-thirty at night. There had to be dozens of other things Adam would rather do on a Tuesday evening. Danielle had broken off their engagement after the car accident. Surely he'd begun to date again in the year that had passed.

"Yes, me." He raised a brow at her incredulous tone. "I'll enter a series of admission orders in her medical record while you get started."

"Of course." To her relief, Adam chose not to use the computer in the room but left to head to the nurses station.

She stared at the empty doorway for a moment, remembering the time he'd rescued her from a second date gone bad. She'd called Danielle to pick her up, but Adam had answered the phone instead because her sister hadn't been feeling well. He'd immediately come to for her, angry at how her date had been a little too enthusiastic about getting his end of the night kiss. She'd been a mess, emotionally so more than physically, and Adam had given her a hug, offering comfort.

She'd known he viewed her like a younger sister, but her feelings for him had morphed into something more that night. Maybe because her track record with men hadn't been very good. She had a tendency to find losers, making it too easy to think of Adam as her knight in shining armor. Thankfully her summer break from college had ended and she hadn't had to face Adam for a long time afterwards. Until two weeks before Christmas.

Before the car crash.

Joy squirmed in her embrace, reminding her she had work to do. She took a moment to nuzzle Joy's downy head with her cheek. Then quickly went to work.

A safe haven baby. She had only heard about them, and knew it was a law that had been put into place to encourage young mothers to give up their babies without any questions asked, or fear of retribution. She wondered why Joy's mother had taken such a drastic action. And about what happened if the young mother changed her mind?

She had no idea.

She set the baby and the procedure table, removed the bright pink sleeper in strapped Joy securely so she wouldn't fall off. Starting IV's on babies was the hardest thing she'd had to learn during her transition to becoming a pediatric nurse.

She managed to place the IV on the first stick, drew one set of blood cultures off the line, and was basking in the glow of her success when Adam returned.

"Have you drawn her blood yet?"

"Yes, one set of cultures off the IV site. I only need one more culture from a different site."

"Good." He watched as she finished dressing the area where the IV was placed. "Doris, my receptionist at the clinic, tried to feed her. But she didn't take much, not even a full ounce."

At six weeks the baby should have been taking at least two to three ounces of formula at a feeding. She frowned. "I don't suppose we have any history from the mother?"

"No." His brow furrowed. "We may want to try a soy based formula."

She nodded in agreement. "Do you want me to draw the second blood sample or would you rather do the lumbar puncture first?"

"Go ahead and draw the second set of blood cultures."

Self-conscious under his watchful gaze, she wished he'd leave. He didn't. Ignoring him wasn't easy, although she thankfully found a scalp vein and managed to draw the second sample without difficulty. She labeled the small tube of blood, quickly matching the ID number on the sticker to that on the small bracelet wrapped around Joy's ankle.

"Will you watch her for a minute so I can get these down to the lab?" She raised her voice to be heard over the sound of Joy's crying.

There was a brief hesitation before Adam nodded and stepped toward the procedure table. "Sure."

Skirting around him, she grabbed the first tiny tube of blood that she'd already labeled, carrying both to the main nursing station. At Children's Memorial, runners hand delivered all blood to the lab, the precious samples were not entrusted to the pneumatic tube system. Once she'd handed them off to the nursing assistant to do the task, she returned to Joy's room.

And halted abruptly, when she saw Adam cradling the infant against his broad chest.

Her heart thudded, her throat squeezing shut.

What was it about a strong man holding a baby that turned a woman to mush? Here she thought the stupid crush she'd harbored for her sister's former fiancé was dead but, no, suddenly, the old feelings had flared back to life.

Somehow, she needed to find the strength to stay away from Adam, so he'd never discover how she really felt.

ADAM DID his best to ignore his odd reaction to Krista. The flash of physical awareness had caught him by surprise. Not because he harbored any lingering feelings toward her sister Danielle but more because he'd always viewed Krista as a kid sister. After all, she was closer to Amber's age than to his.

It was disconcerting to discover the sweet kid had grown into a beautiful woman.

Krista entered the room and began to prepare for the lumbar procedure. He set the baby back down on the procedure table. Krista carefully held Joy in position as he swabbed the baby's back with antiseptic solution, then carefully inserted the spinal needle between the baby's first and second lumbar vertebrae.

When a drop of cerebral spinal fluid appeared at the end of the lumen, he stopped advancing the needle. "Hand me the first tube, would you?"

Krista handed over the small plastic specimen container. He let several drops of cerebral spinal fluid fall into the receptacle before closing the cap and asking for the next one. Once the procedure was finished, he used a sterile two-by-two and withdrew the needle.

Normally he didn't have trouble blocking women from his mind, especially when working. But tonight, he did. Krista smelled like Christmas, a subtle mix of evergreen trees and cranberries. The tantalizing scent distracted him.

She was stunning, with her long dark brown hair pulled back into a ponytail. Her natural color suited her so much better than the blonde dye. Krista was shorter than Danielle had been, the sisters didn't resemble each other much. But the moment he'd looked down into Krista's wide brown eyes he'd recognized her.

He glanced at her again, but she was trying to soothe the crying infant. He must have passed her around the hospital but if so, he hadn't made the connection. She'd been working here all this time? He wasn't sure how he hadn't run into her earlier. Except that they hadn't shared a patient to his knowledge.

Joy's cries were getting weaker. If anything, the IV fluids should be helping to rehydrate her.

"Did you order antibiotics?" Krista asked, reading his mind.

"Yes." He watched as she quickly stripped away the sterile field. "Now that we have both sets of blood cultures drawn, and the LP finished, I'd like her to get the first dose ASAP."

"Of course." Krista gently set the baby in the middle of the crib.

Watching her take care of baby Joy did funny things to

his stomach. He almost wished Joy's mother had chosen some other clinic to leave her baby.

No, that wasn't true. He was glad to be here for the baby. He hadn't consciously avoided infants over this past year since he and Danielle had lost their unborn child, but it had certainly helped to know Phoebe had preferred taking care of the younger ones.

And if Phoebe had been here, he might not have gotten to know Joy. Or Krista.

"She is set for the moment," Krista informed him. She covered the baby with a blanket and raised the bar of the crib even though Joy was too young roll over and fallout. "I'll see if pharmacy has sent the antibiotics yet."

He nodded, unable to tear his gaze from the baby. The car accident had been his fault. His stubbornness had cost his son's life. Holding Joy was a painful reminder of what he'd lost. He knew his secret desire to reunite the baby with her mother wouldn't atone for his sins.

Nothing would turn back the clock, no matter how much he wished he could.

His stomach knotted as he relived those painful moments. The screeching tires, the horrible crash of metal against metal as the semi-trailer had barreled into them. He'd swerved, trying to avoid the contact, but seconds too late. The passenger side, where Danielle had been sitting, had been hit with enough force to deploy their airbags.

Danielle had survived with surprisingly few injuries, but the seat belt across her lap had left bruises. Considering she'd only been four and a half months pregnant, the doctor had prepared them for the eventual miscarriage.

Their relationship hadn't survived the tragedy. No surprise, really, when their rocky relationship had contributed to the loss.

"I have the antibiotic." Krista returned, triumphantly holding a small syringe he assumed was the medication.

"Great." He abruptly realized there was no longer any reason for him to stay. Except to wait for Alec. With the frown he glanced at his watch. He'd hoped his brother would be there by now.

Krista set up the antibiotic, giving him a puzzled glance. "Ah—is there anything else, Adam? I mean, Dr. Monroe. I have things under control if you need to get going."

"You can call me Adam." Leaving the infant in Krista's capable hands would be the sensible thing to do, but since he had to wait for Alec, there was no reason for both of them to stay. Krista no doubt had other patients to tend to. "I don't remember if you know my brother Alec, he's a sergeant with the Milwaukee Police Department and he's supposed to meet me here. I can watch Joy if you have other patients to see."

"Okay." She hesitated in the doorway, glancing back at him. "What will happen to her?"

He shrugged. "I've never personally handled a safe haven baby. I imagine once she's medically cleared, she'll go into foster care until someone adopts her. Unless her mother returns to claim her." And if he had his way, he'd find the mother to give her a chance to change her mind. If she was only giving up the baby for financial reasons, and not as a result of substance abuse or some other behavioral health issue.

Krista frowned, as if she'd anticipated his answer. "It's sad that she'll end up in foster care."

Poignant silence fell and Adam realized he and Krista were completely in tune over the fate of this precious little girl. He wasn't sure why the idea of foster care bothered him so much. The baby's young age practically guaranteed a quick adoption. In fact, he was sure there was a long list of parents just waiting to jump at the opportunity.

Knowing a nice family would take Joy into their hearts and homes should have reassured him. But it didn't. He couldn't shake the sense that Joy belonged with her mother. The baby had been well cared for, despite her illness.

"Let me know if you need anything," Krista murmured as she took a step toward the door.

"I will."

She flashed a quick smile before leaving. Her smile stayed with him for a long moment. For some odd reason he remembered the night he driven out to pick her up from a date who'd gotten too enthusiastic with his attempt to kiss her goodnight. He'd been so angry on her behalf it had taken every ounce of self-control not to plant his fist in the guy's face.

Krista had deserved better.

His phone dinged with the text. Alec was downstairs in the emergency department. He texted the room number so that Alec could meet him up there.

"Hey." He nodded at his brother. "Thanks for coming."

"No problem." His brother's gaze softened when he saw the baby. "I need you to tell me exactly what happened."

"What do you mean? Baby found in waiting room with a note. What else is there?"

Alec gave an exasperated snort. "Details, bro. I need details."

"I don't have details." Adam handed over the note. "Only this."

His brother took it, examining the note closely. "Where was it?"

"Tucked in the side of the infant carrier, like this." Adam demonstrated.

"Hmm. Seems like this was a well thought out plan. She notes financial difficulties as the reason for giving the baby up. I'm not sure what you expect me to do." Alec shrugged. "Joy is a safe haven baby."

"I know that, but I'd still like to find the mother."

His brother stared at him. "The whole point of a safe haven baby is that we don't find and persecute the mother."

"Yeah, I get that. And if we find the mother, and she has substance abuse issues or psychiatric issues then we'll just let it go. But I feel the need to try."

His brother sighed. "We don't have anything to go on."

"Please, Alec. What if this baby was taken by someone?"

"There would be a missing person report." Alec could tell he wasn't going to give up, so he added, "Okay, but be prepared to be disappointed. I have a feeling there's a good reason she left her baby in your clinic."

"I know. I'm grateful for anything you can do." He was secretly relieved Alec had agreed to help. His unborn son hadn't stood a chance, the odds had been stacked against him even before the truck had hit them.

He wanted, needed, things to work out better for Joy.

KRISTA STARED at Joy with a troubled frown. The baby was getting worse instead of better. Joy's respiratory rate impulse had increased significantly, despite the breathing treatments and antibiotics Adam had ordered.

She bit her lip and inwardly debated her next step. Normally, she'd call the mother—if the parents weren't already at the bedside—and then the resident on call. But in this case the only person other than herself who cared about Joy's condition was Adam Monroe.

How did he feel about being called at home? Eleven o'clock at night wasn't horribly late, but he'd only been gone two hours. For all she knew, he'd be irritated at being woken up. She gazed back down at the sleeping infant tucked in the curve of her arm. Should she wait or should she call?

She tried to remain objective when her feelings toward Adam were anything but. Even as she watched, the baby let out a barking cough. That sealed the deal. Joy was getting worse. There was no doubt about it. She'd extended her shift another four hours to cover a sick call on the night shift. And that meant notifying Adam of Joy's change in condition was a necessity.

To her surprise, he'd put a note in Joy's chart to call him at home on his cell with changes in her condition. Holding the baby in the crook of her arm, she quickly placed the call.

"Hello?" His deep voice, husky with sleep made her knees go weak.

She took a calming breath and told herself to stop being an idiot. "I'm sorry to bother you, but Joy is getting worse. Her respirations are up to 48 per minute and her pulse is over 160." She bit her lip, trying not to show the depth of her concern. "She's more lethargic, too. And has not taken a full ounce of formula."

"What's her oxygenation status?" He sounded more awake now. "And how do her lungs sound?"

"Her lungs sound the same, we just finished giving her a breathing treatment. Unfortunately, her pulse ox is still hanging in the low 90s. I think we should try a croup tent."

"Yeah, that's a good idea." There was a brief pause, before Adam added, "I'll be right in."

"No!" The word slipped out before she could catch

herself. "I mean," she hastily amended, "that isn't necessary. I've been keeping a close eye on her. I won't take any chances. If her condition doesn't improve, I'll contact the resident and arrange a transfer to the PICU."

"I trust you, Krista. But it's after eleven. Isn't your shift over?"

"No, I agreed to stay four more hours to help cover the night shift."

"Good." The relief in his tone warmed her heart. "I feel better knowing you're there to watch over her. Her lethargy worries me."

"I agree." The increase in Joy's vital signs could mean the antibiotics were trying to fight off the infection, yet the decreased oxygenation status and her lethargy were bad signs. "Is there anything else you'd like me to do?"

"If the croup tent doesn't work, call me back. She may need to go to the PICU to be intubated."

"I will." Krista knew babies who needed to be intubated at this young age often suffered other adverse effects, like potential damage to their lungs. She hoped and prayed Joy's respiratory status improved so it wouldn't come to that.

"Thanks for calling."

Thank heavens he couldn't see the goofy smile on her face. "You're welcome."

Feeling better, she hung up the phone and quickly arranged for a croup tent to be set up. For it to work, she'd need to set the baby down, which little Joy didn't seem to like much.

Krista's other tiny patients were doing fine, all of them had their mothers present in the room. Except of course for Joy. After the croup tent was set up and Joy was safely nestled inside, she made rounds on her other patients, feeling guilty at how she'd rather be at Joy's bedside.

She tried to rationalize that Joy needed her more because there wasn't anyone else to stay with her. Yet she knew that wasn't the only reason. In the few hours she's been assigned to take care of her, the safe haven baby had touched her heart.

She assessed the baby again after Joy had spent a solid thirty minutes in the croup tent. Joy's respiratory rate came down to 42 breaths per minute and her pulse ox reading went up to a whopping 94 percent.

Progress, but not enough to consider Joy out of the danger zone. A noise outside the door made her jump in surprise. Her elbow jerked, clinging into the side of the crib with a loud clatter. She winced and glanced at Joy sleeping on her back in the tent. Thankfully the baby hadn't woken up.

"Sorry, didn't mean to scare you." Adam stepped into the room, stealing her breath in his well worn pale blue jeans and navy sweatshirt instead of his usual shirt tie and white lab coat.

"I'm fine." At least she would be once her heart got over its momentary lack of oxygen. As she glanced back at the baby, she frowned. Why hadn't Joy woken up when she'd rattled the crib? Worried, she leaned over and touched the baby, feeling for a pulse.

Joy responded to her touch, her tiny fists waving in startled surprise when she woke up. She let out her breath in a silent whoosh. The baby's lethargy didn't seem as bad as before.

"How is she?" Adam crossed the room to stand beside her, gazing down at the crib.

"Better." She quickly logged on to the computer and brought up the graph of Joy's vital signs. "See? Her vitals are responding to the croup tent."

"I'm pretty sure she has RSV so I'm not surprised." He leaned closer to review the information on the computer screen. Then he took a step back and tucked his hands into the pockets of his jeans. "If we can get her through the night, I'm sure she'll be better by tomorrow."

She nodded, shooting him a sidelong glance. "I thought you trusted me?"

The corner of his mouth kicked up in a half smile. "I do. I tried to go back to sleep but couldn't. Figured I was better off here, helping you."

She smiled, even though the last thing she needed was to spend the next few hours in close contact with Adam.

She liked him far too much already.

CHAPTER THREE

An awkward silence fell as they both watched baby Joy sleep. Krista bit her lip and tried to think of something to say. It seemed as if they were both avoiding any mention of her sister. She was more than a little curious as to how he felt about their broken engagement.

"Krista?" Jenny one of the night shift nurses called loudly into the room. "We're getting something to eat from the cafeteria. Did you want something?"

"No, I'm fine." She swung toward Adam grateful for something inane to talk about. "What about you? Are you hungry?"

"No, thanks." He smiled and she found herself staring at the way his eyes crinkled at the corners.

Stop it, she admonished herself. This was ridiculous. He was being nice, courteous as they took care of a very sick baby.

Her gaze dropped the monitor where are the babies pulse ox and heart rate readings flashed on the screen. Joy had fallen back asleep. Gazing at the baby, she couldn't shake the feeling that something wasn't right. Joy hadn't moved a bit when Jenny had called her name or when she dropped her stethoscope earlier that evening. Thinking back through her shift, Krista realized Joy only responded to being touched or held.

Grabbing the stethoscope from around her neck, she threw it loudly to the floor without taking her eyes off Joy.

"What are you doing?" Adam jumped at the loud clatter reverberated through the room. "Trying to give me a heart attack?"

Krista swung around to face him, her eyes wide. "She didn't move, Adam. Not a single bit. I think Joy is deaf."

ADAM STARED AT KRISTA, wondering how she'd figured out something he—as the pediatrician had missed. "Deaf," he repeated. "That would explain a lot. No wonder she always quieted down when someone held her. She couldn't hear voices to know someone was near."

"The poor thing," Krista murmured. "I wonder if her mother figured it out?" Her gaze collided with his. "Do you think it's the reason she abandoned her?"

"No." Adam didn't want to think the worst. He knew there were some horrible parents out there, he'd reported a couple child abuse cases over the past few years. But he hadn't seen any unexplained bruises or injuries when he'd examined Joy. The mother's note led him to believe she would have mentioned the deafness if she had known. She had after all mentioned Joy's fever. "I'll order more testing so we can discover the extent of Joy's hearing loss. Maybe it's not as bad as we're thinking."

"Maybe," Krista agreed, but her tone was full of doubt. "Guess my talking and singing was all for naught."

He had to laugh, remembering how he talked to Joy in the car on the ride over. "Mine, too."

Krista's expression turned troubled. "Adam, if her mother doesn't come back, Joy's deafness could affect the likelihood of her being adopted."

His smile faded. "Yes, I know. She could qualify for a cochlear transplant, but they won't do the surgery until she's at least twelve months old." Even then he doubted Joy's mother could afford the procedure. Despite financial help from government-based programs, there were potential ongoing costs which may not be covered. Anything from specialist care to simple battery replacements.

Krista tapped her fingers on the TV remote. The television itself wasn't on, but there were several radio stations that could be tuned into. "I guess I don't need to play Christmas songs for her."

It was on the tip of his tongue to agree—he didn't need more reminders of Christmas. But her wistful expression confirmed his suspicion that Krista had put the music on as much for herself as for baby Joy. He knew what Krista and Danielle's lives had been like after they'd lost their parents. Danielle had told him how they'd ended up being shuffled from one relative to the other. No one had wanted them on a permanent basis.

Maybe holiday music reminded her of happier times.

"Leave it on." He could put up with the Christmas tunes, for her sake.

A shy smile tugged at the corner of her mouth. "Okay, I will."

Staring at her, he realized he'd come in tonight for more than just double checking on Joy.

Despite his desire to forget about the past, he'd come to see Krista.

THE NEXT MORNING, Krista overslept. So much for her plan to get some Christmas shopping done. After taking a quick shower, she pulled on a clean set of scrubs with a bright colorful Christmas tree pattern and had just enough time to grab something to eat before she needed to leave for work.

Staring down at her bowl of cereal, she wondered how Joy had fared through the rest of her night. Adam had left about the same time she had, at two o'clock in the morning. He'd insisted on walking her to her car.

Of course, he hadn't kissed her goodnight or anything but for a moment there when he'd gazed intently down at her, she thought he might.

Unless that hadn't been nothing more than her imagination working overtime. She sighed and took a spoonful of oatmeal. She really needed to get over her feelings for Adam. Especially as she didn't know how he felt about her sister. There had to be a non-threatening, casual way to mention Danielle. She hated the idea of Adam pining away for Danielle for a whole year. Her sister hadn't said much about her breakup with Adam, except to say they were fighting a lot and didn't have the same goals for their future.

And if that had truly been the case, Adam couldn't still be in love with Danielle.

Could he?

Had Danielle ever mentioned *her* crush to Adam? She sincerely hoped not. She grimaced. How embarrassing.

Krista knew Danielle had been shaken up after their car accident. Krista had been away at school when it had happened and as far as she knew, Danielle had only spent one night in the hospital for observation. By the time Krista had discovered what had happened and rushed back to Milwaukee, Danielle had already been discharged home. Her sister had made arrangements to move to London within the week.

Krista hadn't seen or spoken to Adam again. Until now.

Enough brooding over the man. Even if Adam was over Danielle, he no doubt still thought of her as a younger sister. Now that she'd let her hair grow out, lost a few pounds and had laser surgery on her eyes, men did tend to notice her. Still, it wasn't as if she had dozens of men lining up to ask her out. She watched women flirt and often wondered why she couldn't seem to master the art.

Maybe it was Adam's fault. She couldn't send out those, *I'm interested* vibes because she'd always measured other men against him, finding all others seriously lacking.

She forced herself to finish her breakfast, then rinsed her dishes and grabbed her purse. She'd spend so much time thinking about Adam she had less than fifteen minutes to get to work.

She ran down the hall of her apartment building, not wanting to be late. The tedious job of scraping ice off her windshield while the frigid wind blew against her face cost her an additional few minutes.

As she walked onto Six South with one minute to spare, she noticed a bustle of activity halfway down the hall, a few feet away from the nurses' station.

Not Joy's room, thankfully, but Krista hurried over to see if her peers needed help.

"What's going on?" She entered the room to find two nurses standing over a baby lying in a crib.

"Denny has been vomiting for the past hour," Wendy said a small frown furrowing her brow. "Come here, Krista. Do you smell something funny?"

She stepped forward and nodded. "Yeah, something sweet. You better call Denny's doctor. The baby should be tested for ketoacidosis."

"That's what I thought," Wendy admitted. "Would you do me a favor and call Dr. Monroe? I don't want to leave the baby alone and his mother went home for a while."

"Sure." She hurried back out to the nurses' station and asked for Adam Monroe to be paged. He returned the call in less than a minute. "This is Adam Monroe. Did you page?"

"Yes, this is Krista. Wendy asked me to let you know that Denny Gibson, the baby in room 612, has been vomiting for the past hour. His breath smells sickly sweet and we think he might need to be tested for DKA."

"Absolutely," Adam agreed without hesitation. "Draw a basic chemistry panel and send it STAT. I want those results as soon as possible."

"Okay." She pulled up Denny's chart to enter the order. "Anything else?"

"Not at the moment." There was a slight pause before he added, "Krista? Keep a close eye on him. If Denny really has DKA as a one-month-old then he has a very serious underlying illness."

She'd heard of cases where young infants had severe acidosis to the point where they suffered a cardiac arrest and died. But she'd never taken care of a patient like that herself. "Maybe we should transfer him to the PICU."

"I'm in clinic and only have one more patient to see. As soon as I'm finished here, I'll head over. Draw the blood and we'll take it from there."

He was right, there was no need to panic yet. But she was still nervous as she hung up the phone. With a hurried step she returned to Denny's room to help Wendy. By the time she'd gotten Denny's blood drawn, the baby had become her patient by default. The rest of the second shift nurses had made out the patient assignments, giving her only two babies for now, Joy and Denny, leaving her open for the first admission.

Both were Adam's patients. What were the odds? For six months she hadn't taken care of any of his patients—now she had the only two patients of his on the entire floor.

Thank heavens Joy was doing fairly well at the moment. Krista knew Denny would need most of her attention. Wendy gave her a quick report, explaining how Denny's mother had gone home to arrange childcare for an older sibling. Krista was very afraid Denny would end up in the PICU before the poor woman could return.

"Krista, the lab is on line one."

She picked up the phone. "This is Krista Vaughan."

"We have a critical bicarbonate level on Denny Gibson. His bicarb is 9.0."

"Really? 9.0?" She repeated the value as she logged into the computer. She knew a bicarb of 9.0 was a dangerously low level. Denny definitely had severe acidosis. "Why don't you give me the rest of the lab results too?"

The lab tech ran down the rest of the basic chemistry results. As soon as Krista finished, she typed the results into a page that she sent directly to Adam.

Her phone rang a second later. "I'm on my way in, "Adam said. "I asked one of my partners to cover my last patient for me. Thanks for sending me the labs. I saw the critical bicarb value and the significant anion gap." He paused then added, "Stop all Denny's feedings until further notice. I want you to start bicarb drip and check his urine for ketones."

"I understand." Using a scrap piece of paper she wrote

everything down, worried she'd forget something important. She wanted to ask what he meant by the anion gap, but there wasn't time.

Adam arrived less than ten minutes later. "How is he?"

"Denny tested positive for ketones in his urine." She stepped aside so Adam could log into the bedside computer. "What underlying disease do you think he has?"

"Propionic acidosis, which is also known as propionyl CoA carboxylase deficiency," he answered absently, reviewing all the lab results.

She had no idea what that was, but it sounded serious. She made a mental note to look it up when she had more time. "What exactly should I be looking for, other than acidosis?"

He glanced at her, his expression grim. "Signs of central nervous system depression for one thing, sepsis for another. I should have gotten an ammonia level too."

"I can have that added on to the previous basic chemistry panel we drew," she assured him.

"Thanks. If it's as high as I think it is, we're going to need to transfer Denny to the pediatric ICU."

She made the call to the lab as Adam continued to examine the baby. His serious expression concerned her. He almost looked sick to his stomach.

"This disease, this propionic acidosis, what sort of prognosis are we looking at?"

"Pretty bad," Adam admitted. "With this illness, Denny's body is unable to metabolize certain proteins and amino acids normally. It's a hereditary disease, passed along through recessive genes." His troubled gaze met hers. "I've never seen a patient survive."

She sucked in a quick breath. "Oh no. His poor mother."

"Yeah." He sighed and dragged his hands down his face. "I need to talk to her as soon as possible."

She did not envy him that task. "She should be back any minute. I can stay with you while you talk with her."

"Thanks." He straightened and examined the baby again. He double checked as if to make sure for himself that she had the bicarbonate infusion going.

Feeling horribly helpless, she stared down at the sweetly innocent baby with the devastating disease. She couldn't even imagine how it would feel to lose a child so young.

Losing her own parents had been bad, but she felt that losing a child must be worse. Much, much worse.

"I need to check on Joy." She edged to the door, fighting tears. "Her breathing has been better, but her fever was still high the last time it was checked."

His gaze sharpened with interest. "How high?"

"Still hovering at about 38.9 degrees Celsius which is still 102 degrees Fahrenheit."

He nodded thoughtfully. "I'd hoped it would have come down by now. Have you been notified of any results yet from her cerebral spinal fluid? I don't see them in the chart."

"No, but sometimes they take twenty-four hours."

"Okay. I'll stay here with Denny while you check on Joy."

He obviously didn't feel comfortable leaving Denny alone. Not that she could blame him. She was worried about the baby herself, half hoping the infant would need to be transferred to the pediatric ICU. She'd never lost a young patient in her short career and didn't want to start today.

Joy was crying when she went into the room, but immediately quieted down when she picked the baby up.

"I'm here, little one." She stroked her finger down the baby's cheek. "What's the matter? Are you finally hungry?"

The way Joy squirmed in her arms and gnawed on her fist, she suspected it was time to try the bottle of formula again. She would have loved to feed the baby herself, but Denny's condition worried her, so she called for one of the nursing assistants to help.

After she had safely handed Joy over to the nursing assistant, Rachel who was more than happy to sit and feed the baby, she headed back to Denny's room.

"How is Joy?" Adam asked.

"Good. Our nursing assistant, Rachel, is feeding her."

"I'm glad. I hope she turns the corner soon." The satis-faction in his eyes dimmed as he glanced down at Denny. "Will you call the lab and ask about that ammonia level? I'm worried he's getting more lethargic."

"Of course." She picked up the phone and called the lab. In less than a minute she had the ammonia level. "It's high at 65."

"That's what I was afraid of. Normal is less than 20." Adam frowned. "We can't delay, he needs to get to the PICU."

"I'm on it." Unable to hide her relief she quickly called the pediatric ICU and the admitting department to let them know about the transfer. As she and Adam were rolling Denny's crib down the hall, his mother arrived.

"What's going on?" She asked in alarm.

Adam glanced at Krista and she nodded, understanding his unspoken request. "I'll take Denny over so you can talk to her."

"Thank you." Adam took Mrs. Gibson's arm and led her into a quiet corner. Krista could hear the woman sobbing behind her as she continued rolling Denny's crib down the hall.

Thankfully the pediatric ICU was located right around the corner from Six South. Denny wasn't the first patient she'd transferred to critical care, but he was by far the sickest.

She did her best to give the attending physician an accurate report and Denny's condition. "Dr. Monroe is talking to Denny's mother, but his main concern is lethargy with a serum ammonia level of 65. We've had Denny on a bicarb infusion for almost an hour, we have not yet rechecked his basic chemistry panel."

The attending physician nodded. "What's his anion gap?"

Rats, she should have asked Adam to explain it to her. "I'm not sure," she confessed. She took out her scribbled notes. "Here are his chemistry results. Adam thought the anion gap was significant."

"Yeah." He glanced at the numbers then nodded. "Yes, 18 is pretty significant all right. Okay, we're going to need to intubate this little guy."

She stepped back, watching as the team of pediatric ICU nurses and doctors took over Denny's care. A few minutes later Adam brought Denny's mother in, too. With Mrs. Gibson between them, Krista and Adam offered support until her son had been intubated.

"I need to call my husband," Mrs. Gibson whispered.

Krista kept a supporting arm around her waist as they crossed to the nearest phone. After Mrs. Gibson placed the call, they were allowed in to see the baby. Denny looked so defenseless with the breathing tube in his throat. The critical care nurses took Denny's mother under their wing, allowing Adam and Krista to return to the floor.

Sobered by the seriousness of Denny's illness, she fell into step beside Adam as they walked back toward Six South. She couldn't think of a single thing to say that didn't sound trite or placating.

Losing a patient was never easy. Not for doctors or nurses. The grim expression on his face tore at her heart. He was truly upset about Denny, as she was. As they approached Joy's room, she lightly touched his arm. "I'm so sorry Adam."

He stared down in her hand on his arm and then gave a jerky nod. "I know. There are some diseases that we can't fix."

"Yes." Logically she knew he was right. "But that doesn't make it any easier, knowing one of your patients might die."

"You're right. Especially at such a young age. Denny has barely had a chance to live his life." Adam's green eyes glittered with pain. She was taken aback by his fierce expression and the rawness of his tone. "There needs to be a rule—babies should never die."

CHAPTER FOUR

When Krista's eyes filled with concern, Adam mentally kicked himself for allowing her to see his pain. Normally he didn't have a problem keeping his emotions in check but today it seemed he'd stretched his limits. Krista's kindness made it all too easy to let go, even though he knew better.

He glanced at the rather lopsided Christmas tree in the corner of the lounge, not far from Joy's room. The holiday season didn't help—Denny's young face had reminded him too much of his stillborn son.

"Adam?" Krista put her hand on his arm. "Are you all right? Should we go someplace to talk?"

Her earnest expression warmed his heart. He pulled himself together, giving his head a decisive shake. "No, I'm fine. I'd like to check on Joy, she's the bright spot in this day, don't you think?"

She flashed an uncertain smile and dropped her hand. "Yes, I do."

He missed her touch but told himself to get over it as he led the way into the baby's room. Joy was sitting in an infant seat on top of the crib mattress, no doubt because she just finished eating. He logged into the computer to read her chart and noted the amount listed on the intake and output form. "Two ounces." He grinned with a sense of satisfaction. "She's finally taking more nourishment."

"That's wonderful." She headed over to the baby, unbuckling the straps of the infant seat then lifting Joy against her shoulder. "Her breathing is better, too. Looking at the monitor, her pulse ox reading is in the mid-nineties."

"I see that." He couldn't argue with her assessment. For a moment he watched her, noticing how she held the baby with a natural grace. He was struck by how different she was from her older sister. Danielle may have been stunningly gorgeous, but she'd loved going out, dancing and drinking in her quest to have fun. She had not been thrilled about being pregnant with their baby. She'd claimed she wasn't ready to be a mother, that she had her whole life ahead of her. The way Krista brushed her cheek against Joy's soft crown, he couldn't imagine her saying anything like that.

The flash of desire irked him. He tore his gaze from the image of Krista holding Joy and forced himself to review the rest of Joy's medical record. Her blood cultures were back and the antibiotics he'd ordered provided the exact coverage he needed. Her cerebral spinal fluid was clear and there was no sign of infection there, either. Everything was going according to plan.

The baby had turned the corner medically, that was for sure. In a few days Joy would be medically stable for discharge. Assessing her hearing loss may give him a little more time, but he'd have to meet with the social worker. Very soon.

"So how has your family been, Adam?" Krista asked.

He was surprised at the abrupt change in subject. "Fine.

Alec married Jillian back in September, and last April, my sister Amber married Nick." Looking back, he was grateful that he and Danielle hadn't made the mistake of getting married. They'd simply been too different.

In hindsight, it was easy to admit he hadn't loved her. Not the way a man was supposed to love his wife.

The way his father loved his mother.

The knowledge only fueled his guilt. His fault. The accident and everything that had followed had been his fault.

"Ah, that explains why Alec looked so happy when I saw him walking down the hall yesterday."

"He is." Shoving the never ending guilt aside, he tried to focus on something else. Like the possibility of finding Joy's mother. He needed to get in touch with his brother, to see if Alec had any leads. Time was running out and he didn't want the baby to be lost in the foster care system. Especially if she was deaf. There had to be some way to find Joy's mother. To make sure once and for all that foster care was the only option.

"Danielle sent me an e-mail a couple days ago. She's doing really well too." Krista's voice was bright, cheerful. "She absolutely loves her new job in London."

How could they find Joy's mother? Maybe by looking through birth records to see how many baby girls have been born with the first name of Joy. That tactic would only work if Joy's mother had given birth in Milwaukee. And they didn't have an exact birth date to go by either. Preoccupied, he nodded. "Good for her. I'm glad Danielle is happy."

"Really?" Krista's surprised expression made him frown.

"Yes. Really." Did she think he harbored ill feelings toward her sister? He hastened to reassure her. "Danielle and I—we wanted different things out of life. Our break-up was mutual." He didn't miss the roller coaster ride of a relationship with Danielle but he did grieve the loss of their child. The baby hadn't had a chance at eighteen weeks gestation—there had been no way to save him.

He'd wanted a funeral, but Danielle refused. She didn't want anyone to know about the miscarriage. He'd given in, mostly because talking about losing his son had been too painful. So he had never said a word, not even to his family. And from what he could tell, Danielle hadn't told her own sister either. What would Krista think if she knew the role he'd played in his son's death?

"That's what Danielle said," Krista admitted, carrying on the conversation as if he wasn't preoccupied with his guilt. "I miss her, but she's living the life she's always wanted."

Yeah, he could certainly believe that. Danielle hadn't wanted the baby, yet after the miscarriage she'd furiously blamed him for the accident and for the loss of their child. Then she'd ended things with him. He hadn't protested, knowing that there was no way to mend their broken relationship. Besides, she'd been right about how it had been his fault. If he hadn't been arguing with her over the future of their child, he might have seen the truck barreling through the intersection, heading straight toward them.

He should have been able to avoid the crash.

The sound of Christmas music interrupted his troublesome thoughts. Hospital carolers, he realized as their singing grew louder.

Krista carried Joy to the doorway, humming along with the song *Winter Wonderland.* He followed, wondering where she was planning to spend the holiday. He wasn't sure Danielle would fly home from London, since neither of them had been close to their relatives.

Except for the one aunt, what was her name? Betty? Barbara? Beatrice? Yes, that was it, Aunt Bea. He'd met the woman a couple times. Danielle claimed she was the best out of the bunch. He remembered when Krista had asked for his help—she'd been worried Bea had suffered a small stroke and she'd been right. Even as a student her nursing assessment skills had been excellent.

He hoped Aunt Bea was doing better. Would Krista spend a quiet Christmas evening with her aunt? Or did she have to work the holiday? For some odd reason he didn't like to think of Krista spending the holiday alone.

It was all too easy to imagine how much she would enjoy the typical loud, chaotic Monroe family Christmas. Krista would fit in with his family better than Danielle ever had. His parents hadn't liked Danielle much. And he'd known Amber and Andrea hadn't gotten along with Danielle very well, either.

The only downside was that if he invited her over for dinner, his mother wouldn't understand they were only friends. She'd be so thrilled that he'd brought a girl home that she'd start planning another wedding.

Nope, that wasn't going to happen. The last thing he wanted was to become involved in another serious relationship.

They hurt too much.

KRISTA WAS a little disappointed when Adam left minutes after the carolers had finished their song. She understood he was busy. No doubt he'd gone back to the clinic to follow up on his other patients.

Yet even as she admitted a new eighteen-month-old baby, not Adam's patient this time, she couldn't help thinking about him. Even the seriousness of Denny's illness couldn't ruin Krista's cheerful mood. She'd been brave enough to broach the subject of Danielle with Adam and had succeeded in eliminating the awkwardness between them.

Adam hadn't seemed upset when she'd mentioned Danielle. In fact, he'd looked as if he couldn't have cared less what her sister had been up to over the past year.

She was confident he didn't still love her sister.

Yet his reaction after Denny's transfer to the PICU nagged at her. He'd seemed more upset than she'd have expected over the situation. Unless he was just the sort of doctor that took his patients well-being to heart? Maybe. Preparing Denny's mother for the potential worst case scenario couldn't have been easy. Maybe Adam had become a pediatrician because the likelihood of losing his patients was far less than in the adult world. As Krista finished her shift and headed home, she realized there were lots of things about Adam Monroe she didn't know.

She didn't know what had drawn him to medicine, or to pediatrics in particular. She didn't know what his plans were for the future.

There was no reason for her to be so curious about him, but she was. And found herself wondering how she might get to know him better.

THE NEXT DAY she was off work, so she ran dozens of errands, beginning with Christmas shopping. Krista had been designated to buy gifts for all the babies on the unit, spending the money the Six South had contributed. With her arms laden with bags of gifts, many of them for Joy, she didn't see Adam's younger sister, Amber, until she practically ran the woman over.

"Krista? Is that you?" Amber asked, once they disentangled themselves and their packages. "It's been a long time! How are you?"

"I'm great, thanks." She'd attended high school with Amber, but instead of going straight to college like Adam's sister had, Krista worked for several years to earn money for tuition. Her parents had died when she and Danielle had been young, eight and ten respectively. They hadn't thought about practical things like life insurance. She didn't blame them—what young couple expected to die when their car stalled on the train tracks? Losing them had been a horrible tragedy. "I hear you're happily married now to a guy named Nick."

Amber's jaw dropped. "Yes. Who told you?"

Krista laughed. "Adam. I ran into him, taking care of one of his patients at Children's Memorial Hospital."

"That explains it." Amber's smile broadened. "You're a nurse too? So am I. That's how I Met Nick. He's a doctor, a rehab specialist."

"That's great. You look wonderful, Amber. Married life obviously agrees with you." Krista was genuinely pleased. Amber had always been nice to her during those horrible years of high school. When the kids had made fun of her because she hadn't any money for nice clothes, Amber had befriended her anyway. They drifted apart though, after

Amber had gone straight to college while Krista had worked two jobs to save money.

"So, you're working with Adam." Amber's curious tone wasn't lost on Krista.

"Yes, but get that gleam out of your eyes—he thinks of me like a sister." No matter how much she wished he didn't. "We share an interesting patient, though, a baby girl who was abandoned as a safe haven baby in Adam's waiting room."

"I heard about her. Joy, right? Alec mentioned it. Such a sad situation, but I'm sure the baby will be adopted very quickly."

"Maybe not. We think she might be deaf."

"Oh, no, the poor thing." Amber glanced at her watch. "I wish we could do lunch and talk more about this, but I have to run. I promised to watch Shannon, Alec's daughter, and need to be home by noon. Maybe another time?"

"I'd like that." Krista smiled and hefted her bags once again. "Take care."

"You too. Keep in touch." Amber took off at a fast pace, clearly running late.

She moved more slowly, mentally reviewing her list. When she passed a bookstore, she stopped, then quickly darted inside.

Meandering her way down the aisles, she finally found what she was looking for. A book on sign language. Even if Joy did qualify for a cochlear transplant, there was no guarantee that procedure would work. Whoever eventually adopted Joy would have to learn sign language and to teach it to the baby as she grew older, to facilitate communicating with the little girl.

Krista bought the book, adding the item to her numerous bags. She made her way out of the mall, trudging through the slush to her car parked what seemed like miles from the entrance.

At home, a small one-bedroom apartment she'd moved into after Danielle had taken off for London, she spent time wrapping the Christmas gifts she'd purchased for the children. Then took the book on sign language and looked through the pictures explaining simple words and phrases.

Although she knew there was a very real possibility Joy's mother could return to claim the infant, she couldn't shake the idea of possibly caring for the baby herself. She'd have to finish the process of becoming a foster parent first, and she also knew the full adoption process took time. Yet she'd applied to be a foster parent two months ago, because there had been a baby whose mother had been severely ill and hospitalized for months. Krista had hoped to temporarily care for the baby, just until the mother was released from the hospital. But it turned out her services weren't needed. And she hadn't completed the process.

Now, she wished she had. She didn't like the idea of sending Joy into the foster system.

After their parents had died, she and Danielle had ended up in a foster home. It had not been a great experience. The woman who had opened her home to them had many children and hadn't bothered to learn any of their names. Instead, she'd used nicknames based on how they looked or acted. The woman had referred to Krista as mouse, because of her mousy brown hair, while Danielle had been dubbed the Wild Child. One of the other kids were called Red, because of a bright head of red hair, Goldie, because of having blonde hair, etc. The woman hadn't physically hurt them or anything, but she had demanded countless chores be done, not the least of which consisted of the older kids taking care of the younger ones.

Krista hadn't minded, but Danielle in her typical fashion, had rebelled. Thankfully the foster home hadn't lasted long, but then their relatives had started fighting over who had to take care of them, shunting them off from one house to the next. It had taken two years for them to land with Aunt Bea, who had wonderfully accepted them for who they were.

She knew what it was like not to be wanted. To be considered a burden. And she did not want Joy to ever feel that way.

Glancing down at the book, she mimicked the hand gestures and began to practice the alphabet.

A, B, C, D...

ADAM COULDN'T SEEM to get Krista out of his mind. The next day, he spent a full eight hours at his pediatric health clinic before dashing to the hospital to make rounds on his patients. He was disappointed he didn't find Krista in Joy's room. After he'd finished, he'd returned to the clinic to catch up on paperwork. The long, empty evening stretched ahead of him.

How had he missed Krista? And why had not seeing her, ruined his evening?

His parents had asked him to stop by for dinner, and he decided to go, mostly because he appreciated a home cooked meal, and needed to see how his mother was coming along.

Two years ago, Alice Monroe had broken her hip and although she was healed and moving independently, he was still a little worried about her. She'd slowed down over the past two years, walking carefully as if her joints ached. He'd mentioned the possibility of arthritis to Amber's husband, Nick, who had agreed that she should probably be seen.

But being the stubborn woman she was, his mother refused. Living with doctors and nurses was annoying, she'd claimed. They were always seeing one illness or another when nothing was wrong. She was absolutely fine.

He didn't believe her, but what could he do? Force her to be evaluated? Even if he'd wanted to do that, he didn't think her primary care doctor would move forward with a consult without his mother's consent.

There wasn't anything else he could do except make sure to step in frequently and to watch her closely for himself.

When he'd finished checking lab results and radiology reports, making his final notes in the various electronic medical records of his patients, he stood and worked the kinks out of his back. If he didn't watch out, he'd be the one with arthritis he thought grimly. The office was empty as everyone else had gone home. That wasn't unusual. Out of the three partners in his practice, he was the only single guy in the bunch. There had never been a reason for him to rush home.

Thinking of his empty condo reminded him again of Krista. Considering he'd once viewed her as a younger sister, she was occupying his thoughts more than she should.

So what if she was empathetic, kind and considerate? So what if she was beautiful in a quiet, down to earth way? She deserved someone better, a guy who would love her and marry her. Give her a family. He'd watched her with Joy—she was definitely a woman who wanted a family.

And he was a man who wasn't willing to get involved in a complicated relationship again.

Scowling, he pulled on his leather coat and gloves

before heading outside. His clinic had a back door for the staff, and he pulled it shut behind him, making sure it was securely locked. December and Wisconsin was cold and dark. As he walked around the corner of the building, he saw a woman standing in front of the pediatric health clinic door, her face pressed up against the glass.

Curious, he stepped closer. What was she looking at? She must have noticed his reflection in the glass because she suddenly spun around, giving him a quick impression of a woman's pale, wan face surrounded by a dark blue scarf, before she hurried off in the opposite direction.

"Hey!" He wondered if she'd come because she thought the clinic was still open. "Are you okay? Do you need medical help?"

The mystery woman acted as if she didn't hear him. He started off after her, but then stopped when she went straight to the bus stop. She rubbed her bare hands together and blew into them as if to warm her fingers.

She was alone. She hadn't brought a child to the clinic to be evaluated.

The bus lumbered forward and she quickly hopped on. He turned walked back to his car, the cold wind cutting through his coat. It wasn't until he had the car warmed up and had pulled out onto the highway that he considered the odd encounter in more detail.

The woman had been wearing a thin coat, considering the temperature outside was well below freezing. She'd had the scarf tucked around her face, but her fingers had been bare lacking the protection of gloves. She dressed as if she didn't have much money, and she couldn't have owned a car, as she'd gone straight to the bus stop.

Why had she been peering into his clinic?

Was it possible she was Joy's mother?

CHAPTER FIVE

Adam wished he'd thought to use his cell phone to get a picture of the woman for Alec. He mentally reviewed her description as he headed toward his parents' house for dinner, knowing Alec would want details.

After parking his car on the street in front of his parents' home, he strode inside and found his family gathered in the kitchen. "Hi Mom, Dad." Crossing over, he gave his mother a hug and a kiss, scanning the room for Alec. "How are you?"

"Good." She flashed an easy smile, and he was glad to note she didn't look strained or exhausted.

He raised a brow, searching her expression for the truth. "Are you sure? How's your hip? Giving you any pain?"

"No pain. My hip is fine. Look, Austin has surprised us with a visit, too." His mother seemed thrilled to with the prospect of cooking for so many of his siblings. "Abe." She turned to his father, a large, gentle man who was the rock in their family. "Take everyone into the living room and get them something to drink, won't you? I have hot apple cider if anyone is interested. Dinner will be ready in half hour or so."

"You heard your mother." Abe's deep voice boomed through the kitchen. "Let me know what you want to drink as always there's a variety of soft drinks to choose from if you're not interested in hot apple cider."

"Cider sounds great to me." Dismissed from the kitchen, Adam clapped his younger brother Austin on the back as they followed their father into living room. "Hey, I haven't seen you in months. How's the smoke-jumping?"

"Going as well as can be expected." Austin didn't smile and the expression in his brother's eyes reflected his somber mood. "The fire in Esperanza is finally out, at least."

Austin had trained as a firefighter and paramedic, but for the past two years had been working on the smoke-jumping team fighting wildfires in California. Adam could tell something had happened, but a crowded room didn't seem the appropriate time or place to ask.

"Where's Alec?" He took the mug of hot cider from his father's hand.

"He can't make it." Amber spoke from her perch on the arm of the sofa where her husband was seated. "Shannon has a cold, so he and Jillian are staying home." Amber leaned into Nick when he wrapped an arm around her waist. "By the way, Adam, guess who I ran into today?"

Hiding his disappointment over Alec absence, he arched a brow. "Why don't you just tell me instead of making me guess?" He wondered how soon he could call Alec to let him know about the mystery woman.

"Thanks Abe," his mother said as she entered the living room and accepted the mug of cider from his father. He was glad to see there was no hesitation in his mother's gait. Maybe she really was doing better after all.

"Krista Vaughn." Amber's tone was light, teasing. "She told me she's a nurse at Children's Memorial and that she's working on an interesting case with you, Adam. That safe haven baby you told us about."

"Oh." He took a hasty sip of his cider and winced when he saw his mother's eyes widen, gleaming with interest. "Krista is a nice kid."

"Kid?" Amber's eyebrows rose with barely repressed indignation.

Nick groaned and shook his head. "Now you've done it," he muttered.

"Excuse me?" Amber's voice rose as she continued, "Krista and I went to high school together, so you better rephrase that. We are not kids. We are women."

When Krista had touched his arm, the tingle that had shot through him had made him keenly aware of her. Not that he wanted his family to know anything about that. He tried again. "Hey, that's my point—you're both the same age. You're my kid sister. Krista has always been like a younger sister to me."

"Hrmph." Amber was clearly irritated with him.

"Austin, help me out here," he cajoled his brother.

Austin didn't smile. "I remember Krista, she was a few years behind me in high school. She was quiet and shy, a little plain maybe, with that bad dye job, but she was a sweetheart. Smart, too."

"She's not plain." His automatic denial burst out before he could bite his tongue. Austin was right about the bad dye job, but he decided to keep his mouth shut. He shouldn't be noticing Krista as a woman at all. Why couldn't he keep her tucked in the little sister box where she belonged?

"You'd hardly recognize her, Austin," Amber agreed. "I almost didn't realize who she was at first. She's let her hair grow long and went back to her natural color of chestnut brown. She wears contacts, too, or had laser surgery, I'm not sure which. She's beautiful."

"Hmm, maybe I should give her a call," Austin said pursing his lips. "I wouldn't mind taking her out while I'm home."

What? Adam straightened in his seat, glaring at his brother slouched on the sofa. "She's not the sort of girl interested in a quick fling, Austin. Unless you're moving back home for good?"

"No." Austin's gaze clouded. "I'm only home for the holidays."

Austin had been gone for the past nine months, and it sounded like he'd be heading back to California again soon. Adam frowned, not liking the way his once carefree younger brother seemed to be carrying the weight of the world on his shoulders.

Annoyed with the idea of Austin asking Krista out, he stood and pulled out his cell phone. He walked into the kitchen as he waited for Alec to answer.

"Hey," he greeted his brother. "How's Shannon?"

"Miserable." Alec sighed. "Upset we wouldn't let her come to dinner."

"Tell her Grandma and Grandpa will have another dinner next week. I'm sure Mom won't mind." He cleared his throat and got straight to the point. "I'm calling because I saw a woman peering into the window of Pediatric Health when I left this evening. When I called out to her, she hurried off, heading to the bus stop. I don't know, Alec but I think it's possible she could be Joy's mother."

"Really? Describe her," Alex said.

Adam included every detail he could remember as he

described the woman in the sequence of events. "I guess what bothered me the most was the way she wouldn't talk to me and avoided looking at me."

"Are you sure she just wasn't window shopping?" Alec asked. "Just because she looked as if she might not have a lot of money doesn't mean she's Joy's mother."

"There aren't any retail stores in the building we rent. There's an adult medical clinic, a pediatric clinic, and a dentist office. Do you think she was window shopping for dentures? I'm telling you I think she was Joy's mother, looking into the window to see if I was there with the baby."

"Okay, I'll see what I can do. But remember we don't typically search for the mothers of safe haven babies. We can't treat her as a criminal when she hasn't done anything illegal."

"I know, but thanks. I appreciate your help." Adam disconnected from the call and glanced back to where Amber, Nick and Austin were still talking. His gaze narrowed on his brother. Austin was leaner than he remembered, he'd lost weight over the past nine months. He knew smoke jumping was physically demanding. Emotionally, too, if Austin's shuttered expression was anything to go by.

Had he been serious about asking Krista out? Nah, he couldn't believe that. Then again, why not? Austin looked so somber, it would make sense that his younger brother was looking for an lighthearted evening of fun. Krista was closer to his age. She'd probably say yes.

He couldn't stop imagining his brother and Krista together. If Austin did ask Krista out, she'd probably touch his arm and offer to talk about his troubles, too. Austin would appreciate her comforting presence, may even open up about whatever had happened to him in California.

He didn't like the flash of jealousy that gripped him by the throat and squeezed tight.

Nope. He didn't like it at all.

KRISTA SHOT out of bed when her phone rang. For a moment she stared, disoriented, until she realized she was at home on her day off.

When she recognized the hospital's phone number on her cell phone, she reluctantly answered. "Hello?"

"Hi Krista," Melanie her boss from Six South said. "Do you think you could come in for a few hours? Emily's son is running a fever at the daycare and she needs to go pick him up."

"Uh, sure." She grimaced, knowing she had things to do but unable to bring herself to say no. Especially when their tiny patients needed someone to take care of them. She glanced at the clock, realizing it was later than she'd thought. Almost nine in the morning. "I can be there in an hour."

"Thanks so much." Melanie disconnected from the call.

As she headed for the shower, the remnants of her dream drifted from her subconscious. She'd been in the car with Adam, the night when she'd called home, breathless and crying, desperately needing a ride. Adam had answered Danielle's phone and offered to come get her because her sister had been in bed with a migraine.

His quiet strength and concern had helped her to calm down. After he'd picked her up, he hadn't rushed home but had driven slowly through the streets, gently probing her about what had happened. She'd tearfully explained how

Robert had driven to his place, instead of taking her back to her apartment. When she'd protested, he insisted he'd only forgotten his wallet and would be right back. She'd refused to go up inside with him, but had stood beside his car. When he'd returned, he'd pulled her close for a kiss. At first, she hadn't minded, but then he'd pressed her backward, grinding his mouth against hers. When she tried to break away, he wouldn't let her go. She'd panicked, shoving at his chest and stomping on his foot until he'd finally stopped kissing her. He'd grabbed her by the shoulders demanding to know what her problem was. His tight grasp had hurt so she'd kicked him in the groin and had taken off running.

She felt foolish for allowing things to spiral out of control. Adam had been angry on her behalf, demanding to know the guy's last name and how well she knew him. She'd only gone out with Robert once before and there hadn't been any issue. He was a friend of a friend, but the incident had scared her enough that she'd stopped dating for a while.

Adam had finally driven her home, walking with her up to the apartment she shared with Danielle in giving her a brotherly hug once inside. He'd wanted her to go to the police but she'd refused. Deep down, she felt the incident was partially her fault, that she'd somehow given Robert the wrong impression or she'd simply blown the entire incident out of proportion.

Why she'd dreamed about that night now, she didn't know. Seeing him again in the hospital setting shouldn't have brought back those memories of that night. Adam had been there for her. As protective as a big brother, wanting to beat up the guy who'd hurt her.

Maybe that was it, she thought as she headed to work. She dreamed about that night because Adam had treated her kindly like an overprotective sibling. Her brain was trying to warn her not to make a big deal of the way they shared a few patients. There was no reason to think his feelings toward her had changed.

She'd always liked Adam, more than she should have. The morning after he'd rescued her, Danielle had complained about having to go to dinner at Adam's parents' house. Krista had been angry about her sister's attitude. She knew Danielle had just been mouthing off but felt as if her sister should have appreciated the way the Monroe family was so close. Very different from what they had experienced growing up. And she'd spent the rest of the day stewing over how Danielle didn't deserve Adam.

Enough. Krista tucked to the memories away as she rode the elevator to the sixth floor. The dream had been a stark reminder that their relationship was nothing more than simple friendship.

And wishing for something more was her problem, not his.

"Thanks for coming in." Melanie smiled when she arrived on the unit. "Would you mind taking over Emily's assignment? Joy is one of her patients."

"No problem." Obviously her boss had figured out how attached she'd become to baby Joy. She found Emily and accompanied her colleague in bedside shift report on each of the three patients.

"Baby Joseph has been diagnosed with mumps, he's just shy of two years old. His mother had several older kids at home, and the father is working long hours to make ends meet, so she's not around as much."

They took a moment to examine the baby together, then moved on.

"Brittany is a seven-month-old being evaluated for failure to thrive. Her mother is working but stops by around four o'clock in the afternoon."

They moved to the third room. "Joy is doing very well—her fever is gone, and her cough is getting better. She has auditory testing scheduled for later today."

"Thanks Emily." One of the reasons Krista liked this unit was because there was always a wide variety of illnesses to learn about. In normally the babies weren't so sick although Denny had been the exception. She wondered how he was doing, but didn't want to dwell on the possibility he was already gone.

She'd barely reviewed all her patients charts and the recent orders when Adam strolled in. Her chest tightened when she saw him. He looked incredibly handsome in a shirt, tie, dress trousers and a white lab coat. She prayed her reaction wasn't obvious. "Hi, Adam."

"Krista, how are you?"

"Great. Are you here to see Joy?" She knew he wasn't the attending physician on either of her other two patients.

"Yes, I ordered preliminary auditory testing for her today." He smiled and fell into step beside her as they walked into Joy's room. "I'm anxious to see the results."

"They haven't called for her yet," she said in an apologetic tone. "Do you want me to call down to see if I can get her moved up on the schedule?"

"No need, it's not a big deal. I'm sure you're busy." Adam glanced at Joy. She had left the baby propped upright in the infant's seat, still in the croup tent after she'd taken her bottle.

She felt bad that he'd come all this way to see test results that weren't even done yet. But she also didn't have time to linger. "I need to check on my other patients. Joseph is doing alright, but Brittany didn't eat well this morning."

"Brittany Meyer?" Adam turned to face her. When she nodded, he went on. "I need to examine her, too. My partner is out of town for the day at his wife's grandfather's funeral. I'm covering his patients."

She should have remembered that George Cumberland was Adam's partner. After months of not having any of Adam's patients, it was a little crazy that she seemed to be interacting with him on almost every shift she worked now.

"Would you like to examine Joy first, or go and see Brittany?"

"Joy seems to be doing fine, if you're worried about Brittany, we'd better see her first."

She appreciated how he seemed to trust her professional nursing judgment. "Brittany is in room 620, just down the hall."

"How much nutrition Brittany take this morning?" Adam asked as they made the short trip down the hall.

"Only three ounces, not nearly enough for a seven-month-old. She doesn't like to eat solids at all. Emily tried a little fruit and cereal this morning, but she wasn't interested."

"Hmm." Adam frowned. "When was she admitted?"

"Last evening. I don't think Dr. Cumberland has ordered much in the way of tests for her." Krista approached the crib, dropping the side so Adam could get access to Brittany. The phone on her hip rang, and she turned from him to answer it.

"This is the auditory lab. We're ready for Joy Smith," the woman said.

"Be right there." Krista disconnected and glanced at

Adam. I have to take Joy downstairs. Is there anything you need for Brittany before I go?"

"No, I'm fine. Go ahead, I'm sure I'll catch up with you later."

She nodded and went to fetch Joy. She stayed with the baby through the testing, and by the time she returned Joy to her room, it was close to lunchtime. She checked on Brittany and squashed her disappointment when she discovered Adam had left. He'd entered a series of orders, though, so she quickly went through them on the computer and made a mental list of tasks that needed to be completed. She was late for her lunch break because she took the time to make sure Brittany's IV fluids were started before heading down to the cafeteria.

"Shirley?" She called out to the social worker who stood ahead of her in the line. "Do you mind if I ask a few questions over lunch?"

"Of course." Shirley waited for her to catch up and they found a small table for the two of them. "What's wrong? Is this about Joy?"

"Yes," Krista confessed. She toyed with her grilled chicken sandwich. "Remember a few months back when I applied to be a foster parent for kids?

"I remember." Shirley dug into her cheeseburger with gusto.

"You said it was a six to eight week process to get approved, but as I've already done the paperwork, the classes and the interview, do you think they would push the application through?"

After a moment, Shirley nodded. "That might work. Although if I remember correctly, the one concern they had during your application process was your single bedroom apartment. Has that changed in the past few months?"

"No." She'd forgotten that part. They had strongly recommended she upgrade to a two-bedroom place which would mean a huge increase in rent. The state wanted to be sure that foster kids had their own bedroom. "But I could look into it. Maybe there's something opening up in my building. Joy is still a baby, a newborn. She wouldn't need her own room for a few months yet."

"I hear what you're saying, but the two-bedroom requirement isn't likely to be waived. It would be best if you could at least get on the waiting list for the larger apartment." Shirley gave her hand a quick squeeze. "I'm happy to give you a reference if you need one. And if it doesn't work out, don't worry, we'll place Joy in a good home. Even if she is deaf, I'm sure someone will step up to take her."

"I know." She tried to smile, but her appetite had vanished. Shirley finished her lunch just as her pager app went off. She pulled out her cell phone, grimaced and then picked up the tray. "I have to go. See you later."

Krista followed more slowly. She'd really wanted to take Joy in as a foster baby. And if Joy's mother never returned, she had planned on adopting the baby, too.

But it seemed as if her single bedroom apartment was going to hold her back. Completely dejected, she made her way to the elevators.

"Krista?" A familiar male voice caused her to glance up. Adam came toward her, his brow puckered in a frown. He reached over to take her arm. "What is it? What's wrong?"

"Nothing." She didn't want Adam to know about her financial woes. She wasn't sure what he'd think about wanting to take Joy into her home.

She wasn't rich, quite the opposite. But she could offer the baby an abundance of love.

"Don't tell me nothing is wrong." Adam continued to

stare he, his brow furrowed with worry. "You look just like the night I picked you up after that jerk attacked you. Talk to me. Tell me what's made you so upset."

His sweet concern almost brought tears to her eyes. No one other than her Aunt Bea and Danielle had cared about her the way Adam seemed to.

CHAPTER SIX

It was shocking to realize how well Adam could read her. She didn't necessarily like knowing her feelings were so transparent. Especially when she didn't know very much about him. As nice as he was, he held his inner emotions close, unwilling to share them.

Like after Denny's transfer to the PICU. Something had been bothering him, but he'd refused to talk about it.

He lightly grasped her arm, his green eyes dark with suppressed anger. "What happened? Did some guy come on to you? Or threaten you?"

"What? No, it's nothing like that." Good grief, how embarrassing to know he'd jumped to the worst conclusion possible. She ducked her head to hide her pink cheeks. "Really, Adam, nothing is wrong. I received a bit of disheartening news, that's all."

He held her gaze for a long moment, silently asking what that disheartening news was. Should she tell him? There was no reason to keep her desire to be a temporary foster parent a secret. Yet she was loathe to open herself to his scrutiny.

"Medical emergency, Six South. Medical emergency, Six South."

When the overhead announcement came on, Krista's heart jumped as if someone had poked her with a sharp stick. When Adam's eyes widened in horror, she knew he thought the same thing.

"Joy!"

Adam turned and rushed for the nearest staircase. She followed close on his heels. Adam wasn't part of the medical emergency response team and neither was she, but that didn't stop her from making a valorous attempt to keep up as they took the stairs to one floor and the next.

Her lungs felt as if they might cave from the pressure when they finally reached the sixth floor. They were both huffing and puffing as they burst through the door heading down the hall in time to see a red crash cart being wheeled into a room.

Not Joy's room, thank heavens.

Her step faltered. Brittany's room? No. Oh dear God, no. She pushed her way past the people standing in the doorway to see if Jenny Spritz, the nurse who'd agreed to cover her patients while she went to lunch, was there. Jenny stood at the opposite side of the room, her eyes full of apology.

"What happened?" Krista asked.

"I tried to feed her again and she suddenly turned blue." Jennifer was a newer nurse too, had gone through the same orientation program as Krista. She looked frazzled. "I didn't know what to do."

"Calling a medical emergency was the right thing to do," Adam said. Krista threw him a grateful glance. He wasn't blaming the nurses, like some doctors did. This was the first time any of her tiny patients had arrested and she hadn't even been there. Adam's gaze swept the room. "Who's leading this code?"

"I am." One of the emergency department doctors answered. She recognized him as Dr. Kevin Irvine. "So far we've been able to ventilate with the Ambu bag and mask. We were just deciding whether or not to place a breathing tube."

"I'm covering for the attending physician of record." Adam spoke in an authoritative tone. "Krista, did we get that X-ray I ordered?"

"Yes." Brittany's pulse oximeter reading remained on the low side at 88% despite the assistance of the Ambu bag, so she understood his concern. Her tone was a tad defensive. "I carried out all the orders you wrote before I went to lunch."

Adam nodded and she realized he wasn't really questioning her nursing care. "Thanks." He crossed to the computer in the corner of the room and logged in. "Keep bagging her unless her pulse ox drops below 85 percent."

Everyone fell silent as Adam reviewed the X-ray on the computer. She felt helpless as Kevin Irvine continued to gently breathe for Brittany with the Ambu bag. Was there something she'd missed while caring for the baby? Some subtle sign that may have foreshadowed her changing condition? Something a more experienced nurse may have picked up on sooner?

"She has a severe lung deformity." Adam's voice broke into her thoughts. "Her pulmonary artery is constricted to the point where it looks almost completely obliterated. Krista, get a cardiothoracic surgeon in here ASAP."

She didn't hesitate, calling the operator to request the CT surgeon to respond, STAT. Adam continued addressing the team. "Kevin, she needs to be intubated as soon as possible."

As she waited for the surgeon to respond, she watched as the emergency team worked on Brittany. The phone rang. When she answered, she quickly filled the surgeon in on what was happening. She finished with, "Dr. Adam Monroe would like you to come up as soon as possible."

"Understood." He disconnected from the line.

"Dr. Ben Timmerman is on his way." She tried to keep her voice from shaking. "I'll call to reserve a PICU bed for her."

"Thanks." Adam's gaze was riveted on the team working over Brittany. After arranging for a bed, she glanced at the portable heart monitor over the baby's head. Her stomach dropped when she noticed Brittany's heart rate was rising at a steady rate.

Adam noticed it, too. "Her pulse is well over two hundred. As soon as you're finished with the breathing tube, you'll need to cardiovert her."

"I just need to verify placement." Before Kevin had finished speaking Adam pulled his stethoscope out and was listening to Brittany's lungs. Krista leaned over to place the small end tidal carbon dioxide detector on the end of the breathing tube. "Good color change," she announced.

"The tube is in." Adam removed his stethoscope from his ears. "Get ready to cardiovert."

Dr. Ben Timmerman walked into the room. "What's going on?"

Adam gestured for the surgeon to join him at the computer. "Here's her most recent chest X-ray. It shows a severely constricted pulmonary artery."

Ben Timmerman's expression was grim as stared at the screen.

Krista jumped when Dr. Kevin Irvine shocked Brittany out of her fast heart rate. She felt like a complete failure as a pediatric nurse. She never should have left the unit to go to lunch.

Ben looked up from the computer. "Transfer her to the PICU, I'll call the OR and get a team ready." He frowned, looking over the group gathered in the room. "Where's her mother?"

She sucked in a quick breath. How could she have forgotten about Brittany's mother? "I'll call her." She reached for the phone then turned the computer so she could access the number from Brittany's medical record.

"Hello?" The voice on the other end of the line sounded weary.

"Mrs. Meyer? This is Krista from Children's Memorial calling. Brittany has taken a turn for the worse. She's okay," she hastened to reassure the woman. "But I have Dr. Ben Timmerman here who needs to talk to you." She quickly handed the phone to the cardiac surgeon.

As Dr. Timmerman explained the situation, Krista pitched in to help prepare the baby for transfer. Brittany's mom must have given permission for the surgery because Ben placed another call to the operating room.

"Two transfers to the PICU over the course of four days isn't a very good track record," Adam said under his breath.

She silently agreed. The only bright spot was seeing Denny's name on the whiteboard census of the ICU, which meant he was still hanging in there.

Somehow, she held herself together long enough to get Brittany settled. Bitter guilt coated her tongue and as soon as possible, she turned and escaped the intensive care unit.

"Krista?" She ignored Adam, but he caught up with her

and took her arm. She shrugged him off, knowing she was on the verge of losing control. "Wait, talk to me."

"About what?" She stopped and swung toward him. "I'm responsible for this. I left her alone."

"You didn't leave her alone, you left her in the care of another nurse. You need to eat, too."

She wished she could believe him but knew better.

He pulled her into an empty room and close the door. Her eyes burned with unshed tears. "It will be my fault if that little girl dies."

"That's not true." He pulled her into his arms and heaven help her, she leaned against him desperate to absorb some of his strength. She buried her face in the warmth of his chest and inhaled his comforting, musky scent. "Nothing you did caused her pulmonary artery constriction. If you want the truth, there should have been a better physical examination and follow up prior to her admission. My partner didn't tell me much, just that he thought there might be some bonding issues between the mother and the baby."

"Maybe if I had stayed, I would have noticed her distress quicker." Her voice was muffled against his shirt. "Maybe I could have prevented the respiratory arrest."

He leaned he leaned back then lifted her face with his index finger beneath her chin, forcing her to meet his gaze. His green eyes were full of compassion and understanding. "Brittany needs surgery. Noticing her distress sooner wouldn't have made a difference."

"But—" she started to protest but he surprised her by lowering his head and covering her mouth with his.

Effectively silencing her.

His mouth was warm and she didn't have the strength to

resist. He kissed her gently, as if she were fragile and might break. When she sensed he was easing away she slid her arms around his neck to hang on to the moment for a little longer. For years she dreamed of his kiss, but the reality was so much better than her imagination. Adam tasted wonderful, like a mixture of peppermint and chocolate, two of her favorite flavors.

Finally he looked at his head, breaking off the kiss, breathing deeply. "Krista," he murmured resting his forehead against hers. "We really need to get back to the unit."

The unit. She was working. Or supposed to be. She quickly pulled away, knowing she could get into trouble for being there with him. "Yes. You're right. I need to check on Joy."

"Hang on." He stopped her when she turned away, reaching for the door. Reluctantly she glanced back at him. "I need to know you're okay. Not just about Brittany, but about what just happened. I—didn't scare you, did I?"

Scare her? Did he really think that she was haunted by the past? Her expression softened. "No, you didn't scare me."

"Good." He smiled although she could see uncertainty on his face. "Let's check on Joy."

She nodded, knowing he was being considerate to come with her. Gathering her scattered thoughts, she tried to ignore the tingling awareness skittering across her nerves.

Hiding her feelings for Adam would be impossible if he ever kissed her like that again.

ADAM HELD his physical response in check as he walked to Joy's room. He'd kissed her, right in the middle of an empty hospital room. What was he thinking? He should not have forgotten how she'd once been frightened by a man trying to force himself on her. Ending the kiss had taken every ounce of control he possessed, especially when he'd wanted nothing more than to repeat the entire experience again.

He followed her into Joy's room. Jenny was there, watching over the baby. As Krista hurried forward, he realized his plan to avoid thinking of her as an attractive woman was doomed to fail.

He was attracted to her. No way on earth was he going to stand by and let Austin ask her out. The sooner his brother realized Krista was off limits, the better.

"I'm so sorry." Jenny cast a worried glance toward him. "I didn't mean for anything to happen to Brittany, I swear."

"It's not your fault," Krista assured her. "Trust me, I've been feeling guilty, too. Adam—er—Dr. Monroe convinced me Brittney's problem is her pulmonary artery. She needs surgery to fix the constriction. Neither of us could have prevented it. She was probably born with it." She glanced at him, silently asking for confirmation.

"She was definitely born with it," he agreed. "Sometimes baby adapt to their environments a little too well. Her artery constriction probably became more of a problem once she grew older and more active."

"I hope you're right." Jenny didn't look convinced. "I felt sick the whole time the code team was there. Maybe I'm not cut out to be a pediatric nurse."

"I had the same thought," Krista said in a low tone. "But apart from medical emergencies, I love being a pediatric nurse." He was glad Krista seemed to have shaken off her guilt as she stepped closer to Jenny. "Think about it, does any nurse like seeing their patient take a turn for the worse? Sometimes it happens. It's no reason to give up your career. I think we tend to feel responsible because our patients are young and have their whole lives ahead of them.

"I don't know, maybe you're right." Jenny's expression lightened as she flashed a lopsided smile. "I just felt so awful, as if I let you down."

"You didn't let anyone down." Krista glanced at him and he nodded encouragingly. "I felt bad, too because I left you short handed to eat lunch."

Jenny laughed and shook her head. "We're a pair, aren't we? Both taking responsibility for Brittney's change in condition."

"Yeah." Krista smiled at Joy, who was looking brightly around the room. "Thanks for keeping an eye on her for me."

"You're welcome. This day has flown by, but I'm glad our shift is almost over." Jenny waved a hand toward the hallway. "While you were transferring Brittany to the pediatric ICU, I gave Gretchen report on Joy. You can go home, unless you have something to add."

Adam was glad Krista's grueling shift was over. "Do you know if her auditory results came back yet?"

"I haven't looked for them," Jenny admitted.

"Don't worry, I'll do it." He didn't want to keep the nurse longer than necessary. He crossed the room and logged into the chart. Jenny hovered next to him while Krista picked up the baby and nuzzled her.

"Do you have any other questions, Dr. Monroe?" Jenny asked.

He shook his head. "No, thanks. Go home and have a good evening."

"I'll try." She turned and left the room.

The results of Joy's auditory testing we're not good. Yet he couldn't help but smile as Krista cradled the baby against her chest.

"How are you, sweetie?" She pressed a kiss on the top of Joy's soft head. "I feel as if I neglected you today."

She dropped into the rocking chair, holding the baby on her knees so Joy was facing her. He had noticed Joy was very animated now that she was feeling better, making funny facial expressions while she waved her arms in unco-ordinated movements.

"Aren't you just the cutest thing?" Krista smiled at the baby.

"I'm sorry to tell you, but her auditory test results have confirmed a pretty significant hearing loss, in the ninety percent range," he said with regret. "She can't hear you."

Her startled glance met his. "I thought so. During the test I could see she didn't react to the sounds except for maybe the very highest pitched ones. But I read that it's important to talk to deaf children face to face so they can eventually learn how to lip read. Which is what I'm doing now, right Joy?"

She'd been reading up on deafness in children? He was impressed that she'd taken the time to learn more about what Joy might be facing. He couldn't seem to tear his gaze from the beautiful picture they made together. Yet despite the amazing image of the two of them, he could tell Krista was emotionally invested with this baby. Maybe too much.

"I guess she'll need a cochlear implant," Krista said.

"Yes, when she's eligible for surgery, at twelve months or so." A cochlear transplant was only the beginning. Joy would need extra care, special schools, speech therapy, and so on. Was he doing the right thing to search for Joy's mother? As far as he knew, Alec hadn't come up with anything on the mystery woman outside his clinic. And even if they did find Joy's mother, maybe she couldn't afford all of this. Sure, there were state programs that would cover basic medical care. But would the state insurance for low income mothers go as far as to cover a cochlear implant? He honestly didn't know.

Yet he firmly believed the child needed to be with her mother. The rapt expression on Krista's face bothered him. "Your shift is over, isn't it?"

"Yes. I'm off duty, don't worry. I'm spending time with Joy on my own time." Her defensive tone grated on his nerves.

"I'm not worried about your work ethic, Krista." He frowned. "I'm concerned you're getting too attached to her."

"Joy. Her name is joy." Her defiant gaze met his. "I am attached to her. I had hoped to take Joy into my home as her foster mother."

"Really?" He couldn't hide his shock at the news.

"Yes. A similar situation came up a couple of months ago with a baby who needed a temporary home and I went through the whole application process to be a foster parent. I was close to being approved, but there is one recommendation that I haven't been able to take care of yet." She frowned. "One that might hold me back from having Joy placed with me."

He realized this must have been part of her discouraging news. He didn't know what to say. Should he tell her he may have found Joy's mother? Or wait until he knew for sure. Wait, he decided. For all he knew, Joy's mother wasn't fit to take care of her, anyway.

His cell phone rang and he recognized his brother's number. Did Alec have information? "Hello?"

"Hi, Uncle Adam." Shannon's childish voice made him smile.

"Hi, yourself. How are you feeling?"

"I'm fine. I was fine before, too, but Daddy wouldn't listen to me. He and Mommy ganged up on me and told me I couldn't come to the party." Her indignant tone made him laugh.

"I think you need a baby brother or sister so that one day you can gang up on your parents and even the odds a bit."

"Me, too," she confided. "Anyways, I'm supposed to tell you there's a family dinner at Grandma's house this Sunday. Will you come? Please?"

He knew that Krista was listening to his one sided conversation. Memories of their heated kiss washed over him. He forced his gaze away. "Sure. Tell Grandma I would love to come."

"Goody!" Shannon shrilled in his ear. He pulled the phone away to salvage his eardrum. "Grandma and Aunt Amber want you to bring your friend Krista, too."

"Oh, yeah?" He glanced at Krista and her startled expression confirmed she'd heard her name. Kind of hard not to when Shannon was practically shouting into the phone. "I'll ask her, but she might have to work."

"I hope not, but maybe she can switch with someone?" Shannon knew more about hospital shift work than most kids her age, thanks to her mother who was an emergency department physician.

"I'll ask," he repeated. "Bye, Shannon." He slipped his phone into his pocket and cleared his throat. "I'm sure you heard. You are formally invited to our family dinner this

Sunday. If you're not working and if you're interested in coming."

"I'm off work this weekend." She paused her expression uncertain. Then as if solving some internal debate, she nodded. "That would be nice. I'd love to come."

"Great." He shouldn't feel like a kid who'd just been handed a large Christmas gift, but he did.

CHAPTER SEVEN

Adam didn't see much of Krista over the next few days, just the occasional encounter when he made rounds at the hospital. He'd checked in on Joy, pleased with her progress. The baby would be ready for discharge in a day or two at the most, but he wasn't sure how long it would take to place her in a temporary foster home.

After making rounds, he'd had to go back to the clinic. The flu season had hit with a vengeance, and they had dozens of kids flocking in to seek medical attention. Even though Phoebe was back from her trip, they were so busy he went home late more often than not. On Friday, as he closed down the clinic later than usual, he thought he saw the same woman as before. She was wearing the same dark blue scarf over her head and walking towards the bus stop. He turned up his coat collar against the biting cold wind and headed down the sidewalk to talk to her.

She must have glimpsed him coming because suddenly she wasn't there. He frowned breaking into a run, scanning the crowded streets for her. With only two weeks until Christmas, the area was packed with shoppers laden with bags and packages. He dodged pedestrians, trying to figure out which way she'd gone, desperate to at least get close enough to take her picture.

Twenty minutes later, he was forced to admit he'd lost her. But even as he strode back toward his car, he knew he was on to something. The scarf woman looked guilty, and the way she disappeared to avoid him made him all the more determined to talk to her. She must be Joy's mother. It was the only logical explanation.

He considered Krista's plan to become a foster mother to Joy. While admirable, he wondered if she really understood what she was getting herself into. Babies were adorable, no doubt about that, but they were also a huge responsibility. Especially a deaf infant. His stomach twisted as he remembered the night he'd lost his son. The agony of watching Danielle double over in pain, knowing she was losing their baby yet helpless to do anything to prevent it.

He never wanted to go through that again. Blocking the horrible images from his past, he took a deep breath and stared through the windshield, waiting for his car to warm up, assailed by doubts. Had he made a mistake and inviting Krista to his parents' house for dinner? No matter how hard he tried to convince himself otherwise, he felt as if he was being slowly drawn into something resembling a relationship.

The heated kiss they'd shared still haunted him. Krista deserved someone better, but he hadn't imagined her response to him. She'd kissed him back, there was no doubt about that.

He was tempted to call her even went as far as to pull his phone out of his pocket before he remembered she was working second shift.

Shoving his phone back, he took a hard right to head for

the hospital. There was no reason for him to go back, but he drove in that direction anyway. He wanted to see Krista.

Even if it meant only more heartache for him in the end once she knew the truth.

KRISTA WAS HAVING A BUSY NIGHT. They had an influx of babies with the flu being admitted for dehydration. After she'd started her third IV, she glanced at the clock, wondering how many more patients they could possibly take before the end of their shift. There were only two empty beds, but that didn't mean one of their patients wouldn't be discharged or moved to another floor to make room for more.

To her surprise Adam walked onto the unit, wearing his black leather coat and looking devastatingly attractive. Her heart slammed against her ribs when his gaze sought and met hers. He carried a large white bag. A hint of peanut oil, soy sauce and ginger tickled her nose, making her mouth water.

"Hey, Krista. Do you have time to take a break for dinner?" He held up the white bag.

"Dinner? Chinese?" There had to be Chinese food in the bag. She shook her head with real regret even as her stomach rumbled. "I don't think so, Adam. As much as I'd love to eat, I shouldn't leave the floor right now. We've been flooded with admissions." She didn't want anything to happen in her absence, not like the other day when she'd gone to lunch and Brittany had arrested.

"Brittany is fine," Adam said in that annoying way he had of reading her mind. "She tolerated surgery very well and is recovering nicely in the PICU."

"I know, I checked on her the other day." She had been reassured by the baby's condition. "I still don't think I should leave.

"What if we stayed up here, in the break room?" Adam persisted. "I brought plenty to share. The rest of the nursing staff can eat, too."

He was sweet to understand her dilemma. Relieved, she nodded. "That would be great, thanks. Let me just tell Emily and Jenny I'm taking my break now but then I'm nearby if they need me."

She hurried off and spoke with both nurses, before returning as quickly as possible to the break room. Adam had unpacked all the white containers, filling the break room with the tantalizing aroma of ginger.

"You need to eat," he gently chided as she filled her plate with succulent sweet and sour shrimp over rice. "It's not healthy to skip meals."

Strange to hear him say that. Danielle's appetite had been anything but robust, it was one way her sister had managed to maintain her slim figure. Krista had always eaten when she was hungry, which is why she wasn't as willowy slim like Danielle. "I'm fine. Thanks for bringing this over. Much better than the sandwich I slapped together at home in case we were too busy to go down to the cafeteria."

"Our clinic has been swamped with patients, too." He helped himself to a plate and took a seat across from her. "Thankfully we haven't needed to admit any of our patients."

She wasn't about to mention how she'd been disappointed when none of her new admissions had been from his clinic.

An awkward silence fell. She glanced at him beneath

her lashes, even as she made quick work of her meal. Why was he here? Because he didn't have anything better to do? Or worse because he felt sorry for her? The thought was depressing.

Before she could ask, Jenny rushed into the break room. "Krista? Oliver, my new admission in room 604 is throwing up. Can you help me? I'm worried he'll aspirate."

"Of course. I'll be right there." Jenny left. She sent Adam an apologetic glance as she rose to her feet. "I'm sorry, but I need to go."

"I understand." He stood, regarding her steadily. "I'll see you tomorrow, around six o'clock."

"Great. I'll be ready." Her smile dimmed a bit, thinking about dinner at his parents' house. Shannon's high voice had been easy to hear and she suspected he'd only asked her to go because it would have been rude not to. Was he doing all of this from some sort of misplaced responsibility? Because she was Danielle's sister and he felt as if he needed to take care of her? "Thanks again for dinner."

"My pleasure."

Despite her efforts to push Adam from her mind, the deep timber of his voice stayed with her throughout the rest of her busy shift. Filling her with anticipation for what was yet to come.

SHE AGONIZED over what to wear to meet Adam's parents. And the rest of his family. As she'd been scheduled to work the past three days in a row, she hadn't had time to shop, even if she'd had money to spare on a new outfit, which she didn't.

Difficult decision but saving money for a potential

upgrade to a two-bedroom apartment for Joy won over clothes for herself, hands down.

Glancing at her watch, she realized the afternoon had passed quickly. And she still needed to talk to Mr. Baumgartner, the superintendent of her apartment building. She ran down to the first floor and knocked at his door. He didn't answer. Then she heard banging, and found the older man in the basement, working on the plumbing leading to the washer and dryer.

"Mr. Baumgartner?" She tapped him on the shoulder, knowing from experience he was rather hard of hearing.

"Eh?" He spun around to face her, covering his surprise with a scowl. "What? You shouldn't sneak up on a man like that."

"Sorry." She used her brightest smile. "Do you know if there are any two-bedroom units coming available soon?" She would have loved to have a new place by next week, but that wasn't likely. Yet if a two-bedroom apartment was available she could put money down on it and that may be enough to convince the social work office to give her the benefit of the doubt and grant her permission to be Joy's temporary foster mother.

"A two-bedroom unit?" He glared at her from beneath bushy gray eyebrows. With his rather rotund stature, she was struck by the image of him wearing a Santa suit. He'd be an awesome Santa. If he'd lose the perpetual scowl. "Why? You inviting some no-good young man to move in with you?"

She sighed, refusing to point out that if she were the type of woman to invite a young man to move in with her, they'd hardly need a second bedroom. She didn't have a young man, or had even been out on a date in months.

Well, until today.

"No, Mr. Baumgartner, I wouldn't even think of living with a man." It was true even though she knew her view was old fashioned. "There's an abandoned baby girl at the hospital who needs a place to stay for a short while. I'd like to bring her home with me."

"Oh, yeah?" His eyes narrowed as he glanced at her waist as if checking to see if she was telling the truth or just planning for her own future baby. Good grief, he was acting as if her moving into a two-bedroom apartment with some sort of crime. Finally he grudgingly nodded. "The Olsons told me they were looking for a house. If they find one, their apartment will be available. But I don't expect that to happen until the spring."

Spring was too far away, but she forced herself to smile. "That's good to know. Will you please tell me if anything changes? I'd like to upgrade to a two-bedroom apartment as soon as possible."

"I guess. If that's what you want." Mr. Baumgartner grunted and turned back to his leaky pipes.

She turned and slowly headed back upstairs to her place. Trying not to be too depressed by the news, she stood in front of her closet again. She'd wasted several hours trying on one outfit after another without success. Her dressy clothes seemed too dressy and her casual clothes seemed too casual. It was tempting to just wear her scrubs, pretending she'd just come home from work.

Now she was being ridiculous. She pulled out a pair of black slacks and a Christmas green turtleneck sweater. Tilting her head, she took in her reflection.

Not terrible, she thought. She ran her fingers through her long hair, added a touch of makeup to bring out her brown eyes and highlight her high cheekbones. The one feature she shared with her gorgeous sister.

When her doorbell buzzer rang, she gave a start, knocking her hairbrush to the floor. With a deep sigh, she picked it back up and smoothed a hand over her hip.

Willing her heart to settle down, she hurried downstairs to let Adam in.

———

ADAM'S MOUTH went dry when he saw Krista. How in the world had Austin remembered her as being plain? She was beautiful.

Amazingly, send-your-heart-into-asystole, beautiful.

"Hi Adam, come on in." She stepped back, allowing him into the secured area of her apartment building.

Secure was a misnomer. The lock didn't look very sturdy he thought as he followed her to the second floor. Any man intent on getting in wouldn't allow that flimsy barrier to stop him.

"Can I get you something to drink?" She glanced at him over her shoulder as they went into her apartment. He looked around, not surprised to discover she'd made a home out of practically nothing. The small space was decorated to the hilt for Christmas—a wreath on the door, tiny bells dangling from the curtains over her windows, a decent sized tree in the corner of her living room, branches laden with ornaments. Popcorn and cranberry garland, which he felt certain she'd made herself, encircled the tree.

"No thanks, I'm fine." He slid his hands into his jacket pockets when he saw the mistletoe hanging over her doorway. Maybe if he kept his hands tucked away, he wouldn't pull her into his arms for a kiss. "My parents are serving hot cider before dinner, if you don't mind heading straight over?"

Her bright smile sent a shaft of desire straight through him. Danger, he thought, taking a hasty step back. He was entering the danger zone.

"I don't mind at all." She walked to the small closet and drew out her coat.

He took a deep breath, then stepped forward to take the long, ebony coat from her hands. He held it out for her. The scent of evergreen trees and cranberries weren't just from the tree but seemed to cling to her hair. Did she bathe in the stuff? He settled the coat over her shoulders and then strove for a casual tone. "Ready?"

"Yes, thanks." They left her apartment and walked back down the stairs to the main lobby area he escorted her to his car.

"I'm supposed to say thank you." She turned to face him in the dim interior of the car.

"Thank me?" He raised a brow. "For what?"

"Dinner last night." She flashed him a puzzled look. "Chinese food, remember? Jenny, Emily and the rest of the staff really enjoyed your meal."

"Oh yeah." He had gone home to his empty condo, tossing and turning for hours before he'd finally fallen asleep. Thankfully it hadn't been his Saturday to work the clinic. There was no reason for him to be this distracted by a beautiful woman. "Tell them they're very welcome. It's not a big deal. Nurses bail physicians out all the time."

That made her laugh. "I'm glad you realize it," she said in a teasing tone. "Anyway, it's been totally nuts on the floor the past few nights. We ran back to the break room anytime we had five free minutes to eat. We finally finished everything off by the end of our shift. The night nurses were upset we didn't save them any."

Cold Chinese food? He grimaced. "Glad I could help."

"So, tell me who's going to be at your parents' house tonight?"

Was she nervous about meeting his family? No that didn't make sense. She'd grown up in the same area and had gone to high school with several of his siblings. "You know Amber, she'll be there with her husband Nick. My sister Andrea can't make it, Bethany is sick. You know my brother Alec, he'll be there with his daughter Shannon and his wife Jillian. My brother Austin is home for the holidays, so he'll be there." He slanted her a curious glance, seeking a reaction to Austin's name, but she simply nodded. "You'll like my parents, they're great."

"I'm sure they are."

His parents would love her, too. He cleared his throat and concentrated on driving. The little bit of snow that had fallen made the roads slippery.

He parked in front of his parents' house and took Krista's arm to help steady her as they walked up to the door. He knocked twice then open the door and walked in.

Everyone was already there, though the noise level higher than usual. Like Krista, his mother had decorated for Christmas. Krista's eyes widened for a moment but once he drew her forward and began introductions, she relaxed.

"Mom, Dad, this is Krista Vaughan. Krista, these are my parents, Abe and Alice Monroe."

"It's nice to meet you." Krista shook hands with both of them.

"Krista, it's great to see you again." Amber came forward and enveloped her in a welcoming hug. "I'm thrilled Adam brought you along. Come on come on I want you to meet my husband Nick."

Adam hung back, watching as his made Krista feel comfortable without the slightest hesitation. He'd had reservations about bringing her but, of course, she fit right in. Just like he known she would. He tried not to roll his eyes when his mother sent him a sly wink of approval.

"Krista, I remember you from high school," Austin said as he moved forward to take her hand. "You're prettier than ever."

"Thank you." Krista blushed and Adam sent his brother a warning glance, which Austin cheerfully ignored. Since his younger brother was actually smiling for the first time since he'd been home, Adam let it go.

But if his brother's smile turned into anything more, he was dead meat.

"Something to drink, Krista?" Abe asked in his loud booming voice. "We have hot apple cider, or a variety of other soft drinks."

"Hot apple cider sounds wonderful, thank you," Krista said.

"Good choice." Abe grinned and Adam knew Krista had won his dad over easily. Then again, his dad was a pushover for a pretty face. Except for Danielle. "Adam, will you fetch more mugs from the kitchen?"

"Sure." He walked past Krista, lightly brushing her arm as he passed. She shot him a secret smile and in that moment he knew he didn't have to worry about Austin.

Krista was happy to be there with him. He found the Christmas mugs and carried them back to the living room. Shannon was showing Krista her doctor's bag and explaining how the various instruments worked. He'd heard Shannon talk about how much she wanted to be a doctor but had expected the novelty to have worn off by now. He had to admit, he was surprised it hadn't.

Abby and Nick were talking about the Children's Memorial Christmas ball, where proceeds from the sale of the tickets would go to support medical care for kids in need.

Kids like Joy.

He usually attended, most of the physicians on staff did. He'd planned to go alone as usual, but glancing at Krista, he was struck by the idea of taking her with him.

"She's wonderful," his mother whispered. "I like her."

He did, too, but he didn't want to raise his mother's hopes. Especially when he knew full well his mother had arranged for Shannon to call him and invite her in the first place. "Take it easy Mom, this is our first date. Try not to start planning a wedding yet, okay?"

"I'll try," she agreed, but he didn't believe her.

Alec stood and took Jillian's hand, drawing her up beside him. "Listen up, everyone, we have an announcement to make."

Adam stared at his brother, his smile fading.

"Jillian and I are having a baby! Shannon is going to be a big sister." Alec couldn't have looked happier—he beamed with pride. "Our baby is due sometime the end of June."

"Nice shot, stealing my news," Amber said. "Because Nick and I are expecting too!"

His family erupted into pandemonium. Cheers and good wishes to both of his siblings permeated the air.

His face felt frozen in place. He was truly happy for his siblings, especially Alec. For years Alec hadn't known about Shannon but once he discovered he had a daughter, he'd instantly changed his bachelor lifestyle to make room for her. Amber and Nick would make wonderful parents too.

Watching the congratulations flowing back and forth, his stomach knotted. How would his family feel if they knew he had once been an expectant father? If they knew his stillborn son had died mere days before Christmas?

Pressure built in his chest until he couldn't stand it. Krista was looking at him with concern, but he ignored her.

"Congrats Alec and Jillian, Amber and Nick." He tried to smile but knew he'd failed. Blindly, he turned and walked out of the room, through the kitchen and out the back door without his coat.

Heading straight into the cold winter night.

CHAPTER EIGHT

If she hadn't been sneaking glances at Adam, she would have missed the flash of pain that darkened his eyes moments before he spun on his heel and disappeared into the kitchen. When she heard a door open and close, she hurried after him.

"Adam?" She opened the door leading outside, peering through the snow flurries to find him. With the help from a streetlight on the corner, she could just make out the dark shadow of his broad shouldered frame striding across the yard toward the sidewalk lining the front of the house. He didn't respond when she called his name, so she followed, shivering as the chilly wind cut through her cotton turtleneck sweater.

What had happened? Why did Adam seem so upset about his siblings' announcements? Learning he was about to become an uncle should have been happy news. Maybe it wasn't Alec's and Amber's new baby news that had bothered him, but something certainly had.

For the life of her she couldn't figure out what.

"Adam!" She broke into a run, her feet slipping a little

on the snow-covered sidewalk. At least picking up her pace helped keep the blood flowing. It was freezing out here, she really wished she'd had time to grab her coat. "Wait up!"

He turned to see her rushing toward him and stopped. He hung his head for a moment before turning and retracing his steps to meet her. He caught her close in a hug but the way he rubbed his hands over her arms and back told her he was only trying to keep her warm. "What are you thinking? You shouldn't be out here without a coat."

She refrained from pointing out the obvious, that he wasn't wearing one either. She clenched her jaw to prevent her teeth from chattering. "What's wrong? Why are you out here?"

He wrapped an arm around her shoulders and headed back toward the house. "Come on, we need to get you inside before you get chilled."

She didn't argue, even though he hadn't answered her question. She ignored the tiny flash of hurt caused by his unwillingness to confide in her. Once again, he was shutting her out, refusing to talk about his emotions. It was the same thing he had done after Denny's transfer to the PICU, but this was worse. After they reached the back door leading to the kitchen she paused, looking up at him. "Are you sure you want to go back inside? Would you rather leave?"

"I'm fine." His smile was strained. "I just needed a moment alone. My mother would be upset if we left before dinner. Besides, I'm hungry."

He opened the door and she stepped into the warmth of the Monroe family kitchen with a tiny sigh of relief. Glistening snowflakes dotted Adam's dark hair and she wished again he'd confide in her, explain what was going on beneath that calm facade of his.

Thankfully none of the Monroes seemed to have

noticed their brief disappearance outside. Or, if they had, they didn't mention it as the family prepared to sit down in the dining room for dinner. Alice brought mountains of food to the table, two hearty pot roasts with gravy, a couple green bean casseroles and a huge bowl of small red potatoes. Somehow she wasn't surprised to learn Alice had made warm apple cobbler for dessert.

She subtly tugged at the snug waistband of her slacks, thinking it was a good thing she didn't eat like this every day, or she wouldn't fit into her clothes for much longer.

"How is baby Joy, Adam?" Amber asked, sneaking a bite of cobbler from her husband's plate. "Is she still in the hospital?"

"Yes." Adam glanced at Krista. "She is really doing well, and I think she'll be ready for discharge in a few days."

"Baby Joy?" A puzzled frown furrowed Austin's brow. "Is that someone I should know? Or one of your patients?

"A safe haven baby," Alec explained. "Left in Adam's clinic."

"She was sick, but Krista helped nurse her back to health," Adam added. "She had a viral infection but has recovered well."

"Growing like a weed," Krista said with a smile.

"The poor thing," Alice murmured, her expression troubled. "I'm glad God was watching over her by sending her mother to your clinic, Adam."

Krista silently agreed. When Alice stood to begin clearing dishes, she rose to her feet to help. Amber did too and shot meaningful glances at her brothers. "Mom, sit down. We will take care of the dishes." Austin and Adam exchanged knowing looks, then rose to their feet to pitch in.

"Nonsense." Alice ignored her daughter until Adam grabbed the stack of dirty dishes right from her hands.

"It's no use, Mom. Why make us go through the same argument every time?" Adam wasn't taking no for an answer. "We can handle it. Go sit with Dad."

With a sigh, Alice sat. The rest of the siblings jumped up to help, but the kitchen really wasn't large enough for everyone, so somehow Krista and Austin ended up manning the sink to wash and dry dishes while the rest of the clan cleared the table and put the leftovers away.

"Nick bought us tickets for the Christmas ball. Is anyone else going?" Amber wanted to know.

"What Christmas ball?" Austin asked, his hands immersed in a sink full of soapy water.

"It's a charity for Children's Memorial Hospital," Krista informed him. "They always hold it on the weekend before Christmas."

"Really? Sounds like fun." Austin nudged her with his elbow. She glanced at him in surprise. Was he suggesting they should go together? "Krista, I'd love to see you wearing a pretty ball gown."

She arched her brow. "Austin Monroe, are you flirting with me?"

Austin winked, reminding her of his father. It was obvious where the Monroe men had gotten their charm. Abe Monroe was a flatterer, too.

"He'd better not be," Adam said in a low voice. He set a stack of dirty dishes next to his brother and gave him a playful punch in the shoulder. "Not good form to move in on my date, bro."

"Hey, I was just making innocent conversation," Austin protested.

"Innocent? My butt." Adam turned and walked back into the dining room.

Austin flashed a secret smile. "See? It's working. I bet he'll ask you to go."

She rolled her eyes, returning his smile. "Thanks but I don't think I need your help." She would rather Adam asked her to the ball because he really wanted to go with her, not because of some silly adolescent competition with his brother. The fact he'd only invited her tonight because his family had pushed the issue was bad enough.

Cleaning up from the aftermath of their meal didn't take long with everyone's help. Shortly afterwards people began to say their goodbyes.

On the way home, she relaxed in the passenger seat of his car, humbled at how Adam's parents and siblings had welcomed her into the fold. "You have a wonderful family."

"Yeah, I know." He paused, concentrating on the road for a bit before asking, "Speaking of family, how's your Aunt Bea doing?"

She glanced at him, surprised he'd remembered the one family member she truly loved. Her smile was sad. "She passed away a few months ago."

Adam winced. "I'm sorry, Krista. I know you two were close."

"Thanks." She strove for a light tone. "She died peacefully in her sleep, so I can't complain. She wasn't nearly as mobile as she wanted to be after her stroke."

"I remember."

First, he'd rescued her from her disastrous date, and then had taken charge with Aunt Bea's illness. He'd always been her knight, riding to the rescue, but she wasn't satisfied with that any longer.

She didn't need to be taken care of. She wanted a partner, a man to raise a family with. Glancing at his closed expression, she couldn't make herself believe Adam was that man.

He pulled up in front of her apartment complex and kept the engine running as he reached over to take her hand. "You are welcome to come to our house for the holiday. My family would love to have you."

His family? Not him personally? The offer was sweet, but she sensed he was feeling sorry for her because, like Joy, she didn't have any family. Or rather, she had family but didn't much care for them. Her other aunts and uncles had made hers and Danielle's lives miserable. She did have her sister, but Danielle lived on another continent. For all practical purposes, she was alone. Like Joy. The thought was depressing. "Thanks, but I'm working the holiday."

"I understand." He frowned and turned off the car. "I'll walk you up to the door."

An awkward silence fell between them as he accompanied her to the door. She toyed with the idea of asking him in but felt certain he'd refuse as they both had to work the next day.

At the door, he leaned down and brushed his mouth against hers in a light, friendly kiss. She fought the urge to throw herself into his arms. "Goodnight, Krista."

"Goodnight. Thanks for the lovely dinner." Forcing herself to turn away, she unlocked the door and headed inside.

Sleep didn't come easily. She kept thinking that somehow, even though Adam had been kind enough to invite her to meet his family, they were right back on friendship only terms. As if that heated kiss they'd shared at the hospital had never happened.

Other than that brief moment when he'd seemed jealous of Austin's harmless flirting, Adam had treated her as a lonely waif his family needed to adopt rather than a woman he was attracted to.

ON MONDAY KRISTA returned to work, dismayed to discover Joy had taken a turn for the worse. "She's been throwing up for the past couple of hours," Sally informed her during report. "I'm afraid she's come down with the flu."

"We've had more than a few flu patients admitted recently," Krista agreed. "I guess we shouldn't be surprised."

"Dr. Monroe entered an order to start an IV. Do you have time to put it in?" Sally shot a harried glance toward the nurses station." I still need to give report to Helen, too. Jamie Raasch, my other patient, has also spiked a fever and we need to get blood cultures on her."

"No problem." Krista gathered the supplies she'd need and headed into Joy's room. The baby was staring up at the mobile Krista had strung up for her. Joy seemed listless, compared to how well she'd been doing the last time she'd worked.

"Oh, sweetheart," she murmured, picking the baby up and cradling her against her shoulder. "You'll feel better soon, I promise."

She carried Joy to the procedure table and strapped her in. The baby's pathetic cries stabbed her heart and she did her best to ignore the sound as she looked for the best vein to use as a site for the IV.

When she found a decent scalp vein, she prepped the skin with antiseptic solution and then used topical lidocaine on the area so the needle poke wouldn't hurt. She waited for the medication to kick in, then picked up the tiny catheter. Her stomach tightened painfully and her fingers shook as she held the bevel of the needle over the baby's translucent skin.

For a long moment she stared down at Joy, feeling sick to her stomach as a thin bead of sweat trickled down her back.

She couldn't do it.

Despite how she'd used the numbing medicine to prevent the needle stick from hurting too badly, she couldn't do it. Using one hand to slip the cap back over the needle to keep it sterile, she took a step back, watching Joy as she cried from her position on the procedure table. Dear Lord have mercy, what was wrong with her? She'd started numerous IVs in babies—why was this suddenly so different?

She took a deep breath and let it out in a whoosh. Joy needed IV fluids; she could already see the early signs of dehydration. Babies didn't have a lot of body weight, so they were prone to becoming dehydrated much faster than adults. Stealing her resolve, she stepped up to the procedure table again, trying to look at Joy as another patient rather than the baby girl she'd fallen in love with.

"Krista?" Adam's voice startled her. She swung around to find him standing in the doorway. His expression held concern. "Are you okay?"

How long had he been there? Guilt intermixed with embarrassment washed over her. "I just—can't seem to get this IV started."

"Would you like me to do it?" He stepped further into the room.

"Yes." She was being a complete coward, but it couldn't be helped. She waited until he donned a pair of gloves before carefully handing him the catheter. "I appreciate it."

She could hardly watch, biting her lip as the needle

pierced Joy's skin. Once Adam had the needle secure, she held up the end of the IV tubing so he could connect it to the catheter, relieved the procedure was over.

"Thanks."

"Sure." He stepped back and allowed her to remove the baby from the procedure table. "You looked pale for a few minutes there. I hope you're not coming down with the flu, too."

"No, I don't feel sick." At least not anymore, now that the IV was safely in. She held Joy against her chest, an overwhelming feeling of love and caring sweeping over her.

She needed to transfer Joy's care to another nurse. There was no reason she shouldn't have been able to place the IV, other than her inability to see Joy as a patient. She glanced at Adam, hoping he hadn't noticed the truth about her hesitation. "From what Sally told me in report, she's thrown up twice."

Adam nodded. "I stopped here to check on her and the rest of my patients here at the hospital before heading to the clinic. The IV fluids should help. If anything changes give me a call."

"I will." She waited until he had left, before sitting down in the rocker, stealing a few minutes to cuddle Joy close. The baby smelled sweet, and quickly relaxed against her. The thought of handing Joy to some stranger ripped a hole in her heart.

What if her application to become a foster parent was denied? She wanted the baby to be loved and cared for, especially with her hearing loss. What if some inexperienced foster mother didn't understand how to take care of her?

She swallowed hard and pressed a kiss to the top of Joy's

soft head. In the time Joy had been there, the baby girl had taken up residence in her heart.

She forced herself to set Joy back in the crib. After switching patient assignments with another nurse, she found Shirley, the unit social worker.

"Shirley? I haven't heard anything regarding the status of my application."

"No surprise." Shirley gave an apologetic shrug. "The wheels of bureaucracy turn slow. You know it takes a good six weeks to get through the entire process. It's good you had a head start. They're always looking for good foster parents. I'm sure you'll hear from them soon. Probably sometime after the holidays."

"I hope so." Krista forced a smile, hoping surely wasn't just saying that to make her feel better. "I'd love for Joy to live with me. I even have a potential babysitter lined up; in case everything works out." Ms. Granger, one of the widows in the apartment building had agreed to babysit for Joy. The only issue stacked against her was the lack of a two-bedroom apartment, something she hoped at the Department of Health and Human Services wouldn't hold against her.

"Sounds like you have everything planned out." Shirley smiled and patted her arm. "Hang in there. I'm sure they'll be in touch soon."

"Okay, thanks." She turned away wishing she felt as confident. She quickly checked on her patients and gave Jason O'Neil the IV antibiotic he was scheduled to receive.

Once the antibiotic had infused, she disconnected the toddler's IV and lifted him into her arms. At eighteen months, he was a big boy. Healthy and sturdy.

She brought him to the nurse's station to put him in a swing so she could keep an eye on him. After a few minutes though, she wrinkled her nose, realizing he needed to be changed. With the sigh she lifted him back out of the swing.

"Krista?" Adam strode down the hall toward her. He frowned, standing with his hands in his pockets. "According to the patient assignment board, you're not the nurse taking care of Joy any longer."

"No." She smiled sadly. "I guess you were right. I've grown too attached to her. When it came time to put that IV in, I couldn't do it." She shifted Jason on her hip, wishing Adam hadn't observed her failure. "I plan to visit her as often as I can, though."

"I see." He fell into step with her as she headed down the hall, back to Jason's room. "I need to get to the clinic, but I wanted to ask you a question first."

About Joy? She braced herself. "What's that?"

"Will you attend the Christmas ball with me this Friday night?"

Flabbergasted, she gaped at him. Had he asked her because of Austin's meddling? She hoped not. She was already too emotionally involved with Adam, and honestly, with his entire family. It would be better for her to refuse, to put some needed distance between them. She was fairly certain he didn't return her feelings. If anything, he likely felt sorry for her.

The last thing she wanted or needed from Adam was pity.

She willed herself to be strong, but when she opened her mouth, the words didn't come out as planned. "Yes. I'd love to go to the ball with you."

"Great." His warm grin rocked her back on her heels. "I'll pick you up at seven."

"I'll be ready." So much for protecting her heart, she thought as she watched him walk away. Absently untangling Jason's grip on her hair, she wondered if she was wrong about Adam seeing her only as a friend.

The warm expression in his gaze when she'd agreed to go reminded her of their heated kiss. Her lips tingled at the memory.

Maybe attending the ball would prove to be a changing point in their relationship. A chance for Adam to see her as a desirable woman rather than a family less waif.

With determined resolve she decided to stop over analyzing everything. She'd grown a lot during this past year —certainly she had the self-confidence to do this. She even had a red strapless gown that she'd only worn once before, so she didn't need to spend extra money.

One thing was for sure. If Adam still didn't notice her as a woman after attending the ball, he never would.

CHAPTER NINE

Adam knew he'd completely lost what was left of his mind when he spent his limited free time to stand at the bus stop located a few blocks from his clinic. This wasn't going to help him finish his Christmas shopping, he thought wryly. He had plenty of other things to do, rather than hanging out in the doorway of a discount drug store and stamping his feet to stimulate circulation in his toes.

He felt ridiculous, especially as the sidewalks remained crowded with the Christmas shopping rush. People passed in a whirl of motion; it was hard to watch every individual. He could be freezing his feet off for no good reason.

There she was! He straightened, his gaze zeroing in on the woman who stood directly under the bus stop sign. Where had she come from? Did she work somewhere nearby that she always used this bus stop? Or did she keep coming back just to peer through the doorway of his clinic?

Pulling his hat low on his forehead so she wouldn't recognize him and take off running, he shifted his position until he stood in a spot where he could see her better. Keeping his head down as much as possible, he lifted his phone until he could snap a picture. Being this close, he realized she was younger than he had originally estimated, in her mid to late twenties. He could only see her profile but was willing to take what he could get. He took several photos, hoping for at least one decent shot that Alec could use to help discover her identity. When he was satisfied he'd captured her image, he took several steps back, trying to come up with the best way to approach her.

The bus pulled up. No! He was going to lose his chance! She didn't notice him but stood in line to get on the bus, so instead of calling out, he followed the crowd, mounting the steps until he was on the bus too. He hadn't ridden the bus since his college days, but stuffed dollar bills into the slot and passed her with his gaze averted until he found a seat several rows behind her. As the bus pulled away from the curb he sat back hoping he could find out where the scarf woman lived.

He hated feeling like a stalker. Hurting her was the last thing on his mind. If she recognized him, she'd have no way of knowing his intentions were honorable. Slouching low in his seat, he debated calling Alec. As a cop, Alec might be able to talk to her without causing alarm.

Unless of course she was involved in some sort of illegal activity such as drug abuse.

He dialed his brother's number and held his breath waiting for him to answer. When the ringing stopped and his brother's voicemail message came on, he spoke, keeping his voice low. "Alec? Call me. I have information on our project."

Slipping his phone into his pocket, he watched the scarf woman. She didn't interact with anyone but held her purse in her lap and stared straight ahead, not encouraging any conversation. Unlike many of the bus patrons, she didn't wear headphones to listen to music or carry a book to read.

They rode for at least thirty minutes before she stood to get off at the upcoming bus stop. Adam peered through the window. Did she live nearby? He made him note of the street names on the corner, committing them to memory. The scarf woman disembarked from the bus. She was alone so he didn't immediately follow.

He waited for the next step to get off. The wind was cold but at least it wasn't snowing as he turned and briskly walked back toward the corner where he'd last seen her.

The neighborhood was lower class, but it wasn't a slum either. Quite honestly, he expected something worse. She must have been desperate to have given up her baby. Did she have other children? Did she live alone? Or was she living in some sort of abusive relationship?

He was letting his imagination run amok, but he couldn't seem to stop filtering through the various possibilities. Trying to convince himself that talking to the woman wouldn't do any harm, he hunched his shoulders and crossed the street. Once Alec had a name to go with the face, they'd know more about her background. If something was wrong, they'd likely find out from her police record, if she had one. He didn't want to do anything that might cause her more trouble in the long run.

There was no sign of the woman anywhere around the bus stop where she'd gotten off. He scanned the apartment building, wondering if she lived there or in one of the other small and rather run-down houses nearby. There was no way to know for sure.

It was too far to walk back to the clinic, so he waited for the next bus in order to return to the spot where he'd left his car.

He'd send the pictures and the street names to Alec. Maybe with this additional information they'd be one step closer to finding the identity of the mystery woman and hopefully reuniting Joy with her mother.

ON FRIDAY NIGHT, he drove to Krista's apartment. He'd sent the pictures of scarf woman to Alec and his brother had several street cops asking around the area to see if anyone recognized her. There was nothing else he could do for the moment.

Of course, there was the slim possibility his mystery woman wasn't really Joy's mother, but his instincts told him otherwise.

Unfortunately, he hadn't followed his instincts in keeping Krista at a distance. He still couldn't believe he'd asked her to the Christmas ball. After he'd entered Joy's room, to find her staring at the baby with the IV catheter in her fingers, he'd known she hadn't been able to do the procedure even before her stricken gaze had met his. He'd warned her about getting too attached to Joy. He understood though, the baby's innocence had a way of wiggling into a person's heart.

It was less than a week before Christmas and the baby would be medically cleared for discharge soon. Joy coming down with the flu had been a blessing in disguise—it meant she could legitimately stay in the hospital another few days.

And if they didn't have her mother's identity by then, he'd have no choice but to allow the state to place her in a foster home. Joy wouldn't suffer because of a few days in a stranger's care. After all, she was in the hospital now with various caregivers attending to her. He hoped Alec would find Joy's mother. If she didn't have any substance abuse issues and if she was still able to take care of a baby, he'd help her get the resources she needed. The fact that the woman had come to his clinic as if hoping to see the baby, showed how much she still cared.

He pushed the doubts from his mind, straightened his shoulders and went up to Krista's apartment building. He entered the lobby area and pressed the buzzer for her apartment. Instead of releasing the lock and inviting him up, she informed him she'd be right down.

She didn't keep him waiting. He glanced up as she descended the stairs. He sucked in a quick breath at the sight of her wearing a fire-engine red strapless dress that hugged every generous curve. His mouth went dry as she met his gaze.

Boy-oh-boy he was in trouble. She stopped at the landing. Belatedly he noticed she held her long wool coat over her arm. "Let me help." He took the code from her and held it out managing to find his voice. "You are absolutely beautiful, Krista."

"Thank you." She pulled the edges of her coat together and preceded him to the car. He swallowed hard, struggling to find his usual self-control.

He kept the conversation light, despite the way every nerve in his body was attuned to her presence. Her Christmassy scent, pine trees and cranberries, was driving him crazy. "How was your day?"

"Good. Joy is doing better." She smiled. "I checked on her this morning."

He sent her a questioning glance. "On your day off?"

She flushed and nodded. "Yes. I went in to sit with her for a little while. It's hard knowing there isn't anyone in the world who seems to care about her. I hate thinking she might be lonely. She deserves to have a family."

"I know." He reached over, snaring her hand in his. "You care, and so do many others at the hospital. Remember Joy isn't ever completely alone. We are all working together to take care of her."

She nodded and he was glad she didn't pull her hand from his. Krista was going to take it hard when Joy was finally discharged.

He pulled up to the front of the conference center located in downtown Milwaukee, close to the lakefront and handed the keys to the parking attendant. Cupping Krista's elbow and his hand, he escorted her inside.

Many of the faculty physicians from Children's Memorial were there, and he greeted several of them, introducing Krista along the way. Many of the men sent her admiring glances and he found himself wishing she hadn't worn such a stunningly provocative dress.

He frowned. Did she already have the dress or had she bought it recently? A stab of guilt hit hard. He hadn't even considered the cost of a dress when he'd asked her to go with him. Krista made it sound as if she didn't have extra money to spare. Amber was close enough to her size that she could have lent Krista a dress if necessary.

Too late now. Several of the physicians greeted Krista by name. He kept his hand tucked in the small of her back knowing he was acting possessively but unable to help himself. He stayed close, even as they went up to help themselves to the appetizers. There was enough food to feed an army, so they ate and sipped hot apple cider until the band began to play.

Perfect. A slow song. Just what he'd been waiting for.

He set down his glass and gently lifted hers from her fingers. "Will you dance with me?"

She smiled and nodded, holding out her hand. He led her onto the dance floor and drew her into his arms. His heart swelled as she nestled against him. He didn't even care when the band played a Christmas tune, it was worth it to hold Krista in his arms.

Her skin was satiny soft as he trailed his fingers over her bare shoulder. Everyone around them disappeared. It seemed as if he and Krista were alone on the dance floor. He willed himself to stay in control but knew he was in trouble because Krista felt amazing in his arms. He fought the desperate need to kiss her and lost.

"Krista," he murmured, before capturing her mouth with his. He intended to keep the kiss light, gentle, but the moment his mouth touched hers, heat exploded between them.

Oblivious to their surroundings, he lost himself in their kiss. He suspected his feet had stopped moving, giving up the pretense of dancing. Her mouth was luscious, velvety soft and tasted of promises to come.

"Hey, Adam." Amber and Nick shamelessly bumped into them. "Oh, excuse me, did we interrupt?"

He broke off from their kiss, sending his sister a lethal glare over the top of Krista's head. "Yeah. Get lost."

Nick smirked. "Hey, you might want to remember you're in a public place. The heat you guys are generating is enough to radiate through the walls and melt the foot of snow covering the ground outside."

Adam understood his brother-in-law was doing his best to lighten things up. Because even though he wanted nothing more than to be alone with Krista, they were in the middle of a huge ballroom full of people. Amused glances from other couples on the dance floor confirmed that Nick hadn't been the only one to notice his and Krista's embrace. He drew in a deep breath, wondering how many songs he'd missed.

Then Nick's words sank into his brain. "Wait a minute, a foot of snow on the ground? Since when?"

"Since we got here." His sister's knowing grin set his teeth on edge. You'd think a guy could escape his family for one night. "Actually, it's not quite a foot deep yet, but will be soon. Didn't you hear the news? They're predicting at least fourteen inches of snow."

"Are you serious? That's a blizzard." Krista's eyes widened in alarm. "I had no idea that much snow was in the forecast. I didn't bother listening to the news."

Neither had he. He'd kept the radio off to avoid the nonstop Christmas music that had the effect of raking fingernails over every one of his exposed nerves.

"Maybe we should go, soon." He glanced down at her. "Before the worst of the storm hits."

"We plan on leaving early too," Amber confided. She tilted her head, gazing up at Nick. "One more dance?"

"Always." Nick cradled her close as they moved away. His brother-in-law was moving better these days. He'd struggled for months after a serious plane wreck had broken several bones in his body.

Adam didn't trust himself to have one more dance. Krista made his mind spin. Keeping a tight rein on his hormones, he took her hand and walked back toward the buffet tables. "If you're hungry, let's eat something before we go."

"Sounds good." She filled another plate, seemingly enjoying herself.

They took some time to finish eating and then said their goodbyes as they made their way to the door.

Fat snowflakes filled the air, the wind whipping them around in a frenzy. By the looks of the dense white flakes, the blizzard had already started. The streets didn't look too bad, he was grateful to see a large snowplow trundling past. He gave the parking attendant his ticket. When his car arrived, he helped Krista inside and then began the long, torturous ride home.

He kept his speed under twenty-five miles per hour. The streets were slick and visibility was greatly diminished. Twice he almost suggested turning around going back to the hotel to spend the night. Only the fact that they were halfway to her apartment convinced him it would be better to keep going. If his condo had been closer, instead of farther away, he might have suggested going there.

The traffic lights up ahead turned yellow, then red. Gently he tapped the brake, but the car didn't stop. Instead, it slid sideways, hydroplaning on the ice. Krista gasped and clung to the dashboard as he fought to keep the car on the road.

"Adam?" Fear tinged her tone as the car kept moving. He wrestled with the steering wheel, but it was useless. He had absolutely no control. The car hit the curb. With his foot on the brake, and the tired wedged against the curb, the vehicle came to a stop.

For a long second he stared through the windshield. If he'd been going any faster, they may have gone up and over the curb, hitting the brick building of a veterinary clinic.

"A little slippery out here." Krista unclamped her fingers from around the door handle.

"Yeah. Slippery." Visions of the car accident that had cost him his son's life flashed in his mind. It was almost as if a full year hadn't passed. That the accident had taken place yesterday, it was so fresh in his memory. He closed his eyes for a minute forcing himself to remain grounded. Finally, he turned to look at her. "Are you okay?"

She nodded. "You weren't going very fast."

But he'd still lost control. Logically he knew the icy road wasn't his fault. He swallowed hard, shifted into reverse and carefully backed away from the curb. He shifted again and headed back down the street.

This time he crawled at a snail's pace, gripping the steering wheel so tightly his biceps ached with the effort. It took him another eighteen minutes to get to Krista's apartment. He'd never been so happy to see a building in his life.

He threw the gear shift into park and just sat there. Krista seemed to understand, because she waited a minute then reached for the door handle. "You'd better come in." Her expression was serious in the dim light of the car. "There's no way you're driving home in this weather tonight."

It wasn't an invitation for anything intimate. He understood she only wanted to keep him safe. Driving another twenty minutes to reach his own condo would be foolish.

Still, staying with her, even sleeping on her sofa, would only make him want to kiss her again.

CHAPTER TEN

"Thanks, that would be great. I appreciate the offer." Adam's quick agreement to stay on her sofa, knocked her off balance.

"Ah, you should park in the lot, then." She gestured toward it. "You can't leave your car on the street."

"Right. Got it." He backed up and pulled into the parking lot, taking one of the designated visitor spots.

She pushed out of the car, ducking her head as snow pelted her face. Her heart bounced against her ribs like a pinball, as she led the way inside.

Doing her best not to remember the toe-curling kiss they shared on the ballroom dance floor, she took the stairs to her second floor apartment. Adam hovered close behind her. They'd only gotten halfway up, when Mr. Baumgartner appeared at the top of the steps.

"Hi, Mr. Baumgartner," she greeted the elderly caretaker.

The old man scowled at them, and the way he raked his gaze over Adam, made her inwardly groan. She flushed at the barely veiled accusation in the old man's gaze. She did her best to ignore it, it wasn't as if she entertained men in her apartment on her regular basis. And even if she did, her private life was none of the caretaker's business.

"Don't forget to shovel the sidewalk in the morning," he said in a curt tone as they reached the top of the stairs.

"Don't worry, I won't. Have a good night, Mr. Baumgartner." She walked straight to her apartment door and opened it, glancing back to find the older man still staring after her. She waited for Adam to step inside, followed him in and closed the door behind them with a feeling of relief. At least Mr. Baumgartner hadn't embarrassed her.

"You shovel the sidewalk for him?" Adam asked with a frown.

"Yes, he has a bad knee and he knocks fifty bucks a month off my rent in the winter." She shrugged out of her coat and hung it in the tiny closet. Glancing over her shoulder, she watched Adam take his coat off. "Don't you think he'd make a great Santa? We'd only have to find a way to make him smile."

He stepped up beside her, hanging his own coat next to hers. The simple action implied an intimacy she longed for. Irrationally nervous, she stepped back, keenly aware of his musky scent.

"Would you like something to drink?" She ducked into the kitchen. "Coffee? Hot chocolate?"

"Coffee is fine." His expression was thoughtful as he took a seat on her sofa. Because her apartment wasn't very big, she could easily see him from the kitchen. Filling the carafe with water, she scooped grounds into the filter then closed the lid and pushed the button.

"What's wrong?" She crossed over to sit beside him. "You're not really worried about what Mr. Baumgartner thinks, are you?"

"Not exactly." His grin was rueful. "Although he obviously watches out for you in his cranky way, which makes me feel a little better. The security in this place isn't very impressive."

She lifted her brow. "Maybe not, but I'm not helpless. I can take care of myself." It was annoying how Adam was once again treating her as if she were a younger sister he was bound by duty to protect.

"I'm surprised you haven't adopted him as a surrogate father." Adam's green gaze carried a hint of compassion. "Considering how you lost your parents so young."

His astuteness surprised her, because she was rather attached to the elderly man, despite his curmudgeonly attitude. "Growing up the way we did, being shuffled from one relative to the next, was hard. But it did make me appreciate the value of family. I happen to know Mr. Baumgartner lost his wife a few years ago, he had one son who he also lost. He doesn't have any family left. So yes, I do see him as sort of a surrogate father." She grinned and added, "Well, more like a grandfather."

"I see."

She stood and headed back into the kitchen. After filling two mugs with coffee, she carried a small tray containing cream and sugar and set it on the table within reach. "Help yourself."

"Thanks." He picked up one of the mugs and took a sip, drinking it black. She doctored hers with cream and sugar, first. Then relaxed against the cushions.

"Is that why you've become so attached to Joy?" He eyed her curiously. "Because she's all alone in the world, too?"

"I guess so." Staring down at her coffee she wondered how they'd gotten on to such a serious subject. "Most of my life I felt like the odd person out. I was so different from Danielle, and it seemed as if no matter what I did, being good and not causing any trouble, I still didn't belong." She lifted her shoulder and raised her gaze to his. "I love Joy. If her mother comes back and is capable of taking care of her, that's fine. I would never break up a family that was meant to be together. But if, not? I intend to be there for her. Joy deserves to feel wanted. Loved. Safe and secure in the knowledge that she belongs. With me."

"I understand." He set his mug down and reached over to take her hand. His fingers were warm around hers. "But you must realize single parenthood isn't easy. I watched Alec struggle to adjust to being a single dad, once he learned about his daughter, Shannon. The family chipped in to help, but he had to play around his work schedule, going to the graveyard shift just so he could spend more time with his daughter. And he paid a college girl to spend the nights with Shannon while he was working. I can only imagine how much harder it would be with a brand new baby."

She knew he was probably right. Being a single parent wouldn't be easy. She helped care for infants every day, she knew they cried, and fussed and needed constant attention. Yet she felt compelled to take care of Joy, to love the little girl as her own. "I'm sure your brother feels as if the sacrifices were well worth the effort."

"Yes, he does." Adam released her hand to pick up his coffee mug again. "But don't forget, Shannon is his flesh and blood daughter."

A spark of anger burst free. "Are you saying I'd love Joy more if she were my own daughter?"

"No." He hastily backpedaled. "Of course not."

"Because my relatives, my own flesh and blood didn't

love us enough to take me and Danielle into their homes," she continued. "Much less into their hearts. The only exception was Aunt Bea, and we didn't get to live her until the very end."

"Their loss, Krista," he pointed out softly.

Just that quickly, her anger deflated. "Yes. You're right. It was their loss."

"I want the same thing for Joy that you do," he said in a low tone. "A loving family."

She believed him, although she could tell he didn't think she was enough. Maybe he was right. What if there was a young couple, two parents who would want to take Joy into their hearts and their home.

Her heart squeezed in her chest and she reminded herself that the baby may not be easy to place with her hearing loss. They sat in silence for a moment. He sat down his empty mug and patted the cushions. "Thanks for the coffee and for letting me sleep on your sofa."

She took that as her cue to leave. "I don't mind. I feel better knowing you're not driving home in that mess out there."

"Me, too." She felt his gaze upon her as she stood, picked up the tray and carried it into the kitchen. Okay, if she were honest she would admit she was hoping for a repeat of their kiss. But when she told him about her past, about her feelings for Joy and wanting a family, the mood had changed. She didn't think it was her imagination that he'd subtly shifted away from her.

His feelings for her weren't what she'd hoped for.

She headed back into the living room, her step slowing when she discovered Adam had taken off his tuxedo jacket, tie and shoes and was stretched out full length on her sofa, his arm tucked under his head. Yeah, he was definitely putting distance between them.

Hiding the flash of disappointment, she ducked into her room, lifted a spare pillow and blanket from her bed and carried them through to Adam. "I hope the pillow and blanket helps make you more comfortable."

"Thanks." His murmured response sent a shiver of awareness skating down her back.

"You're welcome." She forced herself to turn away. "Goodnight, Adam."

"Goodnight."

For a long time she stared at the ceiling above her bed. She replayed their conversation, and their intense kiss over and over in her mind until she wanted to scream. She didn't think she imagined his response to her on the dance floor. Yet it was just as obvious he planned to do nothing about it.

Why? That was the part she didn't really understand. And was annoyed to realize she hadn't overcome her youthful feelings of inadequacy after all.

ADAM DIDN'T GET much sleep that night, and while he would have liked to blame the short, narrow frame of the sofa, he knew the real reason was because Krista's pillow and blanket smelled like her.

In the bright light of morning, he sat up and scrubbed his hands over his face. He told himself he was glad he hadn't taken advantage of the situation. Yes, he was attracted to her. But emotionally he wasn't sure starting a relationship with Krista would be in either of their best interests.

He needed to tell her the truth about the car accident

and losing his son. Last night he'd almost blurted out the truth but had held back. He had gotten so used to hiding his feelings he wasn't sure how to change. Or even how to segue into the conversation. What was he supposed to say?

By the way, Krista did you know that Danielle was pregnant and we lost the baby the night of the car accident?

Yeah, that sort of thing didn't exactly roll off the tongue.

And he was haunted by the possibility she would be horrified once she learned the truth.

His fault. If he hadn't been arguing with Danielle that night, he would have seen the truck barreling through the intersection straight toward them. There had been time to avoid the crash. Plenty of time to save his son.

That night still haunted him. In the hospital, the nurse had wrapped his stillborn son and asked if he wanted to hold him. He'd taken the baby boy, staring down at his tiny perfect face knowing he'd failed him.

Danielle had cried, turning her face away, refusing to see or hold the baby. He had been inexplicably angry with her for not even looking at their son.

He knew he needed to put the past to rest. Nothing would bring his son back. He had gone through all the stages of grief, even blaming God for taking his son. But he knew the fault was his. He could not let go of his guilt.

Couldn't even bring himself to talk about it.

The fact that he was even tempted to tell Krista had shaken him. The more time he spent with her, the more he liked her. The more he wanted her. Why did it seem that Krista was everything Danielle wasn't?

She was so brave, the way she told him about her past. He really did understand her need for family. He'd almost taken her into his arms to comfort her but hadn't wanted to take advantage of the blizzard.

But he'd really, really wanted to.

With low groan, he stood and padded to the kitchen to make a pot of coffee. Outside the snow had finally stopped and he suspected Krista would be soon heading outside to shovel snow off the sidewalk outside the apartment building.

No way was he going to let her do that chore all alone.

"Good morning." She came into the kitchen, dressed in snug jeans and a cream colored cable knit sweater. "Are you hungry? I have pancake mix."

"Sure." He was more interested in making sure she ate something, so he helped prepare breakfast, enjoying the coziness of her apartment as they ate pancakes sprinkled with chocolate chips.

"I'm sure the roads are plowed by now." She rose and carried her dirty dishes to the sink. "You'll have a smooth ride home."

"I'm not leaving yet." He carried his dishes to the sink too, planning to help her wash them later. "Let's get that shoveling done."

"There's no need," she protested. "It's not a big deal. I do it by myself all the time."

"No argument." He tucked his white shirt into the tuxedo pants, hoping they were strong enough to stand a little snow. The dress shoes would be useless, but he didn't care. With the two of them working together, the job shouldn't nearly take as long. "Let's go. I'm not leaving until the sidewalk is clear."

She rolled her eyes and stomped toward the closet. She rummaged around in there and came up with a spare pair of gloves and a hat. "I don't have boots that will fit you." She eyed his feet. "Although maybe Mr. Baumgartner's boots would work."

"I'll be fine." He wasn't desperate enough to take the old man's boots. He pulled on his coat and the borrowed hat and gloves. Krista looked cute, her long dark hair shiny beneath the red cap. It took every ounce of his self-control not to haul her into his arms for a kiss.

He followed her down the stairs to the back of the apartment building where a tiny shed with yard tools was located. She opened the shed and pulled out two snow shovels, handing one to him.

"I'm surprised Mr. Baumgartner doesn't have a snow blower," he said as they buckled down to work. "Seems like even a guy his age with a bum knee should be able to handle a small snowblower."

"I think he did once, but it's broken. And I volunteered to take over, for a deduction on my rent." Her cheeks were red and she was smiling as she threw a load of heavy wet snow off to the side. "I really don't mind. It's a great excuse to get outside."

He had to agree—there wasn't all that much shoveling to do and the cold, crisp air was refreshing. They worked side by side and companionable silence, finishing most of the sidewalks out back, and then going around to the front.

When the task was finished, he took her shovel along with his and returned them to the shed. As he was closing the door, a snowball connected with the back of his head, sliding with icy coldness down his neck.

"What in the world?" He spun around, expecting to see a couple of kids. Krista giggled uncontrollably, her face radiating guilt. Bending down he grabbed a handful of snow and packed it into a ball. "You're in trouble now," he threatened, taking a step closer. "If you ask my brothers, they'll tell you I always win when it comes to snowball fights."

"Oh yeah?" She swung her arm and another snowball

hit him square in the chest. "Not this time," she shouted, before turning to run.

He took aim and let loose, his snowball striking the center of her back. She let out a squeal and then scooped up more snow, spinning around to retaliate. Her next throw went wide. With a competitive grin he threw another one, hitting her in the side of her head. He felt a pang of guilt when she yelled, "Ouch."

Thankfully she was laughing and gathering more snow, so he relaxed. A snowball came barreling at his head and he ducked just in time to avoid the full blast hitting him in the face.

That had been too close. With a narrowed gaze he gathered up a huge snowball and took off after her. His dress shoes slipped and slid in the snow, but he managed to catch up. Ignoring the cold, he tackled her, taking her down with him into a snowbank.

"Adam!" Her laughter was infectious. He'd planned to wash her face with a fistful of snow but, paused. With snowflakes covering her eyelashes, her cheeks red and her lips parted invitingly, he forgot his original intent. In a heartbeat the playful atmosphere changed into something intense. He lowered his head to kiss her.

So good. She tasted amazing. Her arms wrapped around his neck, pulling him close as she returned his kiss with enthusiasm. He was surprised the snow wasn't evaporating into steam around them. "Krista," he murmured against her lips. "We're getting soaked."

"I don't care." She gazed at him with such desire his legs went numb. Or maybe it was just that his tuxedo pants were soaking wet from lying with her in the snow. Pulling himself together, he levered off her and held out a hand to help her up. He quickly returned to the shed, closing the door securely then took her hand and headed back into the apartment building.

Upstairs, he hovered in her doorway, water dripping off his clothes. "I should probably say goodbye. I—uh, don't want your apartment to get all wet."

She held his gaze as she slipped her coat off, then toed off her boots. "I would offer to put them in the dryer but I don't have anything else for you to wear."

He almost choked at her offer, then realized she was teasing. A ringing phone reached his ears. He patted his pockets, belatedly realizing he'd left it on the kitchen counter.

"It's yours." Krista grabbed it, handing the device to him. "I hope it's not a problem with Joy."

"It's not." There were several missed calls from his brother. He quickly swiped the screen to answer the call. "Alec? What's up?"

"We found her."

"Who?" He couldn't seem to think straight with Krista being so close.

"The scarf woman. Her name is Nancy Williamson and, according to the birth records down at the Milwaukee courthouse she gave birth to a baby girl named Joy Marie Williamson seven weeks ago." His brothers voice held a note of excitement. "You were right. Your mystery woman is Joy's mother."

CHAPTER ELEVEN

Krista held her breath as she listened to the phone call between Alec and Adam.

They'd found Joy's mother?

A mixture of emotions swirled in her chest. Relief, gladness, weariness, apprehension. Of course, the best thing for Joy would be to be reunited with her mother. If her mother didn't have psychiatric or substance abuse problems.

She crossed her arms protectively over her chest as Adam continued speaking with his brother. On one hand, she was thrilled to discover Joy wasn't all alone in the world.

But she couldn't ignore the dread curling in her stomach. She knew better than most, that all homes were not created equal. That the people who were supposed to love and care for children often didn't.

That blood was not always thicker than water.

"I'm sick of taking care of these brats. It's someone else's turn to suffer. I don't care what you think, I'm dropping them off. Today!"

She slammed the door on the painful memory. One of many, although her Aunt Rhonda had been by far the worst.

She'd screamed at them on a regular basis. Slapped her and Danielle across the face several times. And withheld food as a punishment when they did something that made her angry. Krista shook her head, trying to dislodge the buzzing in her ears. She vaguely realized Adam had ended his call with his brother and was looking at her with concern.

"You found Joy's mother?" Somehow, she managed to pull herself together.

"We think so, but we need to talk to her first." His brow furrowed and he took a step toward her. "You look ill. What's wrong?"

"Nothing." She inwardly winced at the defensive note in her tone. "I'm glad you found Joy's mother. Are you going to see her now?"

"Yes, that's the plan." He eyed her warily. "I'm meeting with Alec in an hour. Why?"

She straightened, dropping her arms and taking on a more casual stance. "Good. Because I'm coming with you."

There was a long moment before Adam reached for his coat. "Don't you trust me? I'm not going to hand Joy over to this woman unless I'm convinced doing so would be in the baby's best interests."

Trust him? The notion brought her up short. She did trust Adam. More than she trusted any other man in her life. But that wasn't the point. She needed to meet Joy's mother for herself. She wouldn't be able to rest until she knew for sure Joy's mother really loved and cared about the baby. "I understand, and I do trust you. But I'd still like to come." She hesitated then added, "Please, Adam."

"Okay." He slipped on his coat and took a step toward the door. "Let's go. I just need to run home and change first."

"Great, thanks." She shrugged into her coat and

followed him into the hall. After closing and locking the door behind her, they took the steps down to the first floor.

Outside, they trudged to his car they'd left parked in the small lot behind the building. The freshly shoveled sidewalks reminded her of their brief snowball fight. And how it had ended in a heated kiss. For a few minutes there, she felt as if she gotten closer to the real Adam Monroe.

As she settled in the passenger seat, her stomach fluttered nervously with the anticipation of meeting Joy's mother.

She wished there was time to go and see Joy one last time. To hold the baby close, nuzzling her downy, soft head. To watch her smile as she waved her arms over her head, batting at the mobile strung over the crib.

To kiss her satiny soft cheek, breathing in her sweet baby scent.

Tears threatened and she blinked them back with an effort. This wasn't about her, but about what was best for Joy. Everything was going to be fine. She trusted Adam and Alec to do what was right.

Glancing at Adam's strong profile, she couldn't help remembering how his eyes had darkened with passion when he'd kissed her.

For some odd reason, she felt as if their time together would end once they'd reunited Joy with her mother.

———

ADAM WAS KEENLY aware of Krista sitting beside him as he drove to Alec's house. He'd already gone home to shower and change out of his wet tuxedo. When he'd returned wearing casual jeans and a sweater, he'd found Krista gazing around his condo in awe.

It took him a moment to realize she'd never been to his place. He hadn't consciously kept her out of his home, but the end result was still the same.

He glanced at her, wishing they could go back to the time before Alec's phone call. He couldn't remember ever having so much fun playing in the snow. Couldn't remember ever wanting to kiss a woman as much as he'd wanted to kiss Krista.

Enough. There were more important things to worry about than his tangled feelings toward Krista. After pulling up in front of Alec's house, he let the engine idle as they waited for his brother. Alec's brows shot up with surprise when he saw Krista sitting in the passenger seat but climbed into the back without complaint.

"Hi, Krista," Alec said with a grin.

"Hi." Adam thought her smile was strained as he merged into traffic. She looked nervous about what the meeting. Yet she was the one who'd insisted on coming along.

"Are we heading straight to Nancy Williamson's house?" He glanced at his brother through the rear-view mirror.

"Yeah, it's our best chance of finding her at this point," Alec agreed.

Krista frowned. "You know where she lives?"

Adam cleared his throat. "We know the last known address listed for Nancy Williamson." He decided not to explain about the night he'd followed the poor woman home on the bus. "We honestly don't know if she's still living there or not."

"I see." Krista's expression was troubled. He understood her concern. He was worried about what they would find when they confronted Nancy Williamson, too.

He found the address Alec had provided, a tiny house located a few blocks from the bus stop. He parked alongside the curb and then climbed out, taking in their surroundings.

"Is that a 'For Sale' sign?" Dismay laced her tone.

He had to admit, it didn't look good. The sign hung on a post at a crooked angle, swaying in the wind. The tiny bungalow was in desperate need of a new coat of paint, a few window repairs, and to his inexpert eye, a new roof.

Nancy Williamson had clearly fallen on desperate times. The question was, why?

Drug or alcohol abuse were the most common reasons for financial difficulties. He wondered if they were making a mistake. Exchanging a worried glance with Alec he strode to the front door and knocked.

No answer. With a frown, he rang the doorbell, listening as it peeled through the house. Still no one came to the door.

"Where is she?" Krista asked.

"I don't know." He glanced around at the neighboring houses. "Alec, what do you think?"

His brother shrugged. "The cop who talked to her boss at the discount store said that she had already left for home right after work."

"Are you sure he got the hours right?" Alec had mentioned how Nancy had a job at the discount store located near the bus stop. And he knew it was a short bus ride from here to his pediatric clinic. "Maybe she's working later than he thought?"

Alec sighed. "I don't think so."

"Should we wait?" Krista rubbed her gloved hands together. "It's freezing out here."

"No, we can't stand around waiting." An idea struck. "But we can leave a note. Maybe she's hiding inside the house, scared and worried that we're going to arrest her." It didn't bode well if she was hiding inside, but he didn't see another option. "Do either of you have paper and pencil?"

"Right here." Alec pulled out his small notebook and pen.

Adam wrote a note, trying to keep it short, explaining that Joy was doing very well at Children's Memorial and he wanted to help. He scrawled his name on the bottom and shoved the note into the crack in the door.

He hesitated. What if Nancy really didn't live here anymore and didn't get his message?

"I hope she sees it," Krista's concerned tone mirrored his thoughts.

"Me, too," he agreed.

Alec clapped a hand on his shoulder. "Hey, relax. It's not the end of the world that we couldn't talk to her today. We know her name. We'll find her. Maybe I'll swing by again on Monday."

"Monday?" Krista echoed in dismay. "That long?"

"We'll find her, Alec repeated. She may not live here anymore but we know where she works. Unfortunately, the store manager indicated she doesn't work on Sundays."

"Monday is fine." He jammed his fists in his coat pockets, knowing his brother was right. There was no rush, other than his own anxiety and needing to meet the woman who'd peeked into the windows of his clinic as if to get a glimpse of her baby. He still wasn't sure if he'd done the right thing in tracking her down. Leaving Joy as a safe haven baby, might be better than whatever waited for her in that house.

Krista was quiet as they trooped back to the car. He wished he could say something to make her feel better. Given the way she'd grown up, being sent from one relative's house to the next, he understood her reservations about Joy's mother.

He could tell Krista was a kindhearted soul, a woman who cared deeply for others. He'd caught a glimpse of her compassion when she'd cared for her Aunt Bea. And he also watched her become far too attached to baby Joy—to the point where she hadn't been able to start an IV the infant.

Everything he knew about Krista convinced him she longed for a family. Hadn't she admitted as much when explaining how she'd applied to become a foster parent? Joy wasn't the only baby Krista had fallen for—there had been at least one other, as well. And even if by some miracle from God Joy was successfully reunited with her mother, there was always the possibility of another abandoned baby or orphaned child needing help.

Krista would always make room in her heart for children. Especially children in need. She was the kind of woman who deserved the whole package—a ring, marriage, and a family.

He'd almost had a family once, and still hadn't quite recovered from the loss.

And he wasn't at all sure he was ready to try again.

THE NEXT DAY, Krista was scheduled to work second shift. She didn't start until three o'clock in the afternoon but left her apartment complex early so she could spend some time with Joy.

She walked into Joy's room, half expecting to find Joy's mother had arrived, but the baby was alone in her crib. Staring down at Joy's happy face, she thought about how desolate the house had seemed yesterday with the crooked for sale sign out front. All night she tortured herself with the thought that Joy's mother was living on the street. Curled up somewhere in the freezing cold a week before Christmas.

She hoped and prayed that wasn't the case.

When Joy saw her, she waved her arms excitedly. Krista tried not to put too much stock in thinking Joy could actually recognize her, but still grinned and leaned over to pick up the baby. "Hi there," she crooned, pressing a kiss to Joy's temple. "Are you feeling lonely? I have almost a full hour to spend with you before I start my shift."

She settled into the rocker with Joy on her lap. She turned the baby so that they were facing each other, the way that book on deafness had recommended. She chatted with the baby loving the myriad of expressions that crossed the infants' features. She wished there was more she could do to help Joy begin dealing with her deafness. Had Joy's mother realized the baby was deaf? Despite Adam's assurances otherwise, she wasn't so sure.

It was obvious Joy was feeling better. The baby scrunched her face, making Krista laugh when a fountain of bubbles gathered around her mouth. She was eating better, too. Krista hadn't dared enter the baby's electronic medical record since she wasn't assigned to care for the infant any longer but had overheard the nurses talking about how Joy had actually gained two pounds since she'd first been admitted.

Had it only been two-and-a-half weeks since the night she had Adam had worked together to care for Joy? It hardly seemed possible. Thinking of Adam caused her smile to fade.

She'd bared her soul about her past but she still didn't know very much about him. It was easy to admire his work as a pediatrician, yet at the same time it bothered her the way he held himself aloof. Was he that way just with her, or with everyone? All she knew for sure that was that even when it came to Joy, he managed to keep us safe, professional distance from the baby, never getting too close. He'd even gone so far as to warn her about getting too emotionally attached.

Adam came from a noisy, fun, family, yet she thought it was odd how he hadn't once mentioned ever having children of his own.

He had asked if she trusted him, and she did. But it was clear to her he didn't reciprocate in trusting her. At least not enough to share his hopes, his dreams, or his emotions.

The knowledge rubbed like salt in a wound.

It was time to stop kidding herself. To stop daydreaming about some fantasy future with Adam. He might be attracted to her and had kissed her twice. But he didn't care for her the way she cared about him.

The hour she spent with Joy passed far too quickly. Realizing that it was a few minutes past three, she quickly stood and carried the baby to her crib. "I'll stop back to see you soon, sweetheart," she promised.

She turned away, certain that today was probably the last time she'd see Joy. Even if Joy's mother didn't return, or wasn't capable of taking care of the baby, Adam would likely discharge the baby the following morning. It was obvious Joy no longer needed medical care.

"There you are." Amy glanced up in surprise when she walked into the nurses' station. "We've been worried about you. You're rarely late."

"I'm here." She forced a smile. "Have you already assigned me a few patients?" She fully expected they had. It was her fault she was late, having dawdled in Joy's room.

"Yes, you have a new admission being sent out from the emergency department." Amy handed her a slip of paper. "Megan took report for you. The four-month-old baby was treated with antibiotics for an ear infection and had some sort of allergic response." Amy turned back toward the assignment board. "In addition to that, we gave you the Simmons baby, he's only four weeks old and has a low-grade fever. And your third patient is little Olivia who is having tests for early kidney failure."

All of her patients were babies, but that was fine with her. She preferred them, while many of the others liked caring for toddlers. "Sounds good. When is the new admission due to arrive?"

There was a commotion in the hallway as a crib rolled onto the unit. Amy gestured to it. "I think that's her now."

"Cynthia Downer has a rash covering most of her body, after receiving two doses of penicillin," the emergency department physician, Dr. Luis Garcia informed her. There was a tiny woman, obviously Cynthia 's mother, walking alongside the crib. "I think the main reason Dr. Monroe wanted her admitted was to watch for signs of respiratory failure."

The baby was Adam's patient. After months of not having any of his patients it seemed like they were rolling in nonstop. She needed to learn how to maintain a professional relationship with him unless she planned to quit her job. Which she had no intention of doing.

She loved taking care of kids.

"Thanks for the update." She flashed a reassuring smile at Cynthia 's mother. "My name is Krista, and I'll be Cynthia 's nurse. Let's get her settled into her room, shall we?" She turned and led the way to the empty room next to Joy's. Once the crib was placed up against the head wall where the oxygen and other medical gasses were located, she dropped the side of the crib and began to examine the baby. Dr. Garcia had not been kidding about the rash. She'd never seen such a bright redness covering the entire torso of an infant before.

She pulled out her stethoscope and listened to Cynthia 's lungs. It wasn't easy because the baby started crying. But after a long moment she frowned and glanced up at Luis. "I hear wheezes in both bases."

"Really?" Doctor Garcia took out his stethoscope and listened. His expression turned serious. "Those wheezes were not there before. You better page Monroe."

"Is he on call?" She reached for the phone.

"Yes. Although this patient belongs to one of his partners."

"What's wrong? Is Cynthia going to be alright?" The baby's mother asked in alarm.

"We're doing everything we can," Krista assured her. She asked the operator to page Adam and then glanced at Dr. Garcia. "Would you grab the crash cart before you leave? Just in case I need epinephrine?"

"Good idea." He disappeared from the room.

She turned back to her tiny patient and a very worried mother. "We really need to keep an eye on Cynthia 's breathing. If anything changes, we'll treat her for anaphylactic shock."

Cynthia 's mother bit her lip and nodded. Krista connected a pulse ox sensor to the baby's forehead, getting an initial reading of ninety-two percent A little on the low side, so she used her stethoscope to listen again.

The baby's lungs sounded worse. Even as she watched, the baby's pulse ox dropped lower and lower. The skin around Cynthia 's lips took on a bluish tinge.

It was enough to scare her. She was about to call a code when Adam walked in.

"Thank heavens you're here. She's about to respiratory arrest."

On cue, Luis Garcia rolled the crash cart into the room. She did not waste a second but reached over and cracked the plastic lock off and opened the top drawer to reach for the epinephrine. Then she grabbed the airway kit from the bottom and handed it to Adam.

"I need the laryngoscope," he said.

She locked the laryngoscope blade on the handle and passed it to him. "Do you want me to call the rest of the code team?"

"Yes. In case I have trouble intubating her."

"I'll do it." Luis picked up the phone and made the call.

More nurses entered the room and Krista was glad Amy crossed over to comfort Cynthia's mother.

"Give her 1 milligram per kilo of epinephrine intramuscularly," Adam said.

Estimating the baby's weight from her experience with infants, she didn't hesitate to grab the fleshy part of the baby's thigh and to give the injection.

Adam managed to get the tiny breathing tube placed before the rest of the code team arrived. In moments the room was flooded with even more staff members.

The pediatric anesthesiologist peered at the breathing tube and the subsequently improved pulse ox readings and nodded. "Good job," he said to Adam. "I'll arrange for a PICU bed for her."

Krista felt her own heart rate slowly returned to normal. This was way too much excitement for the beginning of her day. People filtered out of the room, realizing the worst of the emergency was over.

The pediatric anesthesiologist returned. "I'm admitting Cynthia Downer to PICU bed four."

"Thanks." Adam nodded and sent her a look of gratitude. "I appreciate your help, too."

"No problem." There was no denying she and Adam still made a great team. But the moment was bittersweet. This camaraderie between them while working together at the hospital was all that they would have.

She watched Adam explain everything that had just happened to Cynthia 's mother. When the woman began to cry, he put his arm around her and let her sob on his shoulder. She watched them, her chest tight. Cynthia would be fine, thanks to Adam. He was a great pediatrician with so much to give. Too bad he only dished out servings of emotional care to his patients.

She really wished he had some left for his personal life as well.

CHAPTER TWELVE

Krista didn't see Adam again for several hours, although she couldn't seem to stop watching for him. She tried to concentrate on her small patients, who were more than enough to keep her busy.

After obtaining Olivia's urine specimen she sent it to the lab. The baby with suspected kidney failure certainly seemed fine, but the way her creatinine was creeping upward was concerning enough to keep the infant in the hospital until all the testing was complete.

Little Frankie Simmons worried her. He was the one-month-old baby who'd been admitted with a low grade fever. When she had first taken his temperature, it had been 100.8 Fahrenheit. Three hours later, his temperature was up to 102.8.

Holding the baby in her arms, she called doctor strong, Frankie's pediatrician, to inform him of the spike in the boy's fever. He ordered a lumbar puncture procedure to rule out aseptic meningitis. "I'll place the order. Ask the emergency department resident to do the LP and then call me back with the results."

"I will." She glanced down at Frankie, thinking how small he looked. His mother had run home for a few hours to check on her three-year old twins. She debated calling Ms. Simmons to let her know but then decided to wait. The procedure would likely be over before Mrs. Simmons could return to the hospital. And it was probably better this way. Lumbar punctures were not easy procedures for parents to watch.

Adam walked into the nurses' station while she was waiting for Luis Garcia to return her page. She glanced at the clock, surprised to see him this late. It was well past seven in the evening. "You're still here?"

"Yeah." He flashed a tired smile. "Lots of sick kids have been admitted over the past few days. It took me a while to make rounds on all of them."

"I can imagine." Even exhausted, he exuded an attractiveness that made her glance away and swallow hard. Why was she so in tune to his every mood? When the phone rang, she pounced on it. "This is Krista on Six South."

"Luis Garcia. Did you page?"

"I did. Thanks for calling back. I have a 4-week-old infant by the name of Frankie Simmons who needs a lumbar puncture procedure. Dr. Strong would like you to do the procedure for him."

"We're swamped down here at the moment, and we're short a resident because someone called in sick. I'll do my best to get up there, but it may take me a few hours."

"A few hours?" She grimaced in dismay. "For a lumbar puncture?"

"I'm sorry." Luis sounded apologetic. "All I can do is to promise to be up as soon as I can."

"I understand. Thanks." Stifling a sigh, she replaced the receiver.

"What's wrong?" Adam asked.

She smoothed a hand down Frankie's back. The baby was a virtual heating pad. Thinking of his fever only made her more frustrated. "This little guy needs a lumbar puncture, but the ED is swamped. Luis Garcia will come up as soon as he can, but it may take a few hours."

"I'll do it."

She blinked. "You will?"

"Why not? I'm here and have the time."

She remembered the night Joy had been admitted, how Adam had performed her lumbar puncture and then, too. As an attending physician, he certainly had the privileges to do a lumbar puncture procedure. But Frankie wasn't his patient. Was there a rule about this? "I don't know, Frankie's not your patient. I should probably wait until Luis can get here."

"Who's the pediatrician of record?" Adam asked.

"Dr. Ronald Strong."

"I know Ron pretty well. I'll call him. I'm sure he won't mind."

She didn't know what to say as Adam pulled up Frankie's chart on the computer then called his colleague to explain the situation. She couldn't understand why he was being so nice. Surely, he had better things to do on a Sunday night. Especially considering he'd spent a good portion of his day here at the hospital. She would have expected him to be home by now watching football on TV.

When he hung up the phone a few minutes later, he typed on the keyboard. "Ron is happy to have me perform the procedure. I've made a notation in Frankie's chart to cover us in case anyone questions it."

"Adam, why are you doing this?" She glanced around,

making sure no one could overhear them. "Frankie's lumbar puncture isn't your problem."

"I don't like seeing you upset." He offered a crooked smile and the intensity of his gaze made her realize he was doing this for her. And, of course, for Frankie. "Besides, it's not a big deal. Shall we get started?"

"Yes." She wasn't going to argue because she didn't want Frankie to have to wait. She led the way down the hall to Frankie's room and laid the baby in the crib so she could gather the supplies together. Adam helped, arranging the tray the way he liked it. As before, they worked well as a team. After getting everything they needed, she fetched Frankie and secured him to the procedure table.

"What's his latest temp? "Adam asked as he began to unwrap the sterile LP tray.

"102.8, although he feels really warm, so it may be higher by now." She undressed the little guy who cried, not liking his heated body exposed to the air. "Hush, now, it's okay. I'm here for you," she crooned to the baby.

Adam glanced at her but then concentrated on the task at hand. He donned a pair of sterile gloves, then used the microbial solution to watch Frankie's back. She tightened her grip on the baby when he lifted the long, thin spinal needle.

"Ready?" He met her gaze.

She nodded and held her breath, wondering how on earth Adam could find the column of cerebral spinal fluid in such a small baby. But he did, just as he had with Joy, on the first stick.

"I'm ready for the first tube."

She handed him the tubes in order and he put a few drops of spinal fluid into each one. When he finished, she drew in a deep breath of relief. "Thanks, Adam."

"You are welcome." His deep voice reminded her of the fun they'd had playing in the snow. How he'd laughed when she hit him with that snowball and how he'd surprised her when he'd sought revenge by tackling her down into a snowbank.

Mostly she remembered their heated kiss that nearly melted the snow around them.

She forced the images away. This wasn't the time to ruminate over how much she liked him. "Have you spoken to Joy's mother?"

He shook his head. "No, not yet. I stopped by this morning, but she wasn't home."

"She wasn't?" She didn't like the implication of that. "Adam, what if something has happened to her?"

"Try not to think the worst. Will find her."

Maybe they would, but she had a bad feeling the mother would be in no condition to take care of her baby. Selfishly, she hoped that if that was the case, she would be approved as Joy's foster mother. After quickly washing the antibiotic solution from Frankie's back, she dressed him in his light blue sleeper then she cuddled him close for a moment before setting him back in the crib so that she could carry the tubes of cerebral spinal fluid to the lab.

"Do you need anything else?" Adam watched as she labeled each of the tubes with Frankie's name and medical record number.

"No, but thanks. You've been a huge help." She gestured to the baby. "At least I can start the antibiotics as ordered, in case he has bacterial meningitis."

"Sounds like a plan." He glanced around. "I better go. Are you working tomorrow?"

"All week." She kept her tone cheerful.

"I'll see you tomorrow, then." He turned to leave.

She watched him go, wishing she could call him back. As she stood there, she felt more alone than she had when Danielle had moved off to her job in London. More alone, than when Aunt Bea had passed away quietly in her sleep.

She missed the closeness she shared with Adam but wouldn't be satisfied with just a little part of him, either. The small part he chose to share.

She wanted everything. Especially his love.

SHE MANAGED to keep from dwelling on Adam too much as the end of her shift loomed near. She was finishing with Frankie's bath when Luis strode into the room.

"I'm sorry it took me so long," he said. "It was a really rough night. There were back-to-back car accidents involving small kids." His dark eyes held pain. "We lost one of them, a five- year-old boy."

"I'm so sorry." Put in perspective, those trauma victims had needed Luis's help far more than Frankie had. The lines of fatigue etched in the residence face convinced her he hadn't been simply putting her off.

He forced a smile. "Not your fault."

"It is, because I made you rush up here for nothing." She gave him an apologetic glance. "I should have called to let you know I don't need your help with the procedure. Dr. Monroe was here and did Frankie's LP for us. After getting approval from Dr. Strong."

"I'm glad." Luis gazed down at the baby. "I really felt awful about taking so long. It seemed like the stream of patients just wouldn't end. And those last two trauma patients were bad. The little girl is still in surgery, I'm not sure she'll make it."

"Hey, it's okay." She touched his arm, trying to make him feel better. As much as she loved her job, she couldn't imagine working down in the emergency department with trauma patients. Especially small children. "You can head back down and get caught up."

"Yeah, that would be nice." He shook off his somber mood and glanced at his watch. "I only have another hour of my shift left to go. How about you? "

She nodded. "Yep. I'm off at eleven-thirty, too."

"Would you like to stop for a drink after work?" His invitation caught her off guard. Was he looking for someone to talk to after his rough shift? If so, she couldn't blame him. "There's a great Irish pub down the street and they serve hot chocolate laced with peppermint schnapps."

Luis Garcia was a very attractive man, his dark hair and bright smile enough to charm any woman. As much as she wished she could go with him, it wouldn't be fair.

Not when her heart still ached for Adam.

"I'm sorry, but I can't tonight."

He didn't take offense. "I understand. Maybe another time?"

"Sure." If she could find a way to get over Adam, she wouldn't mind seeing Luis away from the hospital. Maybe he didn't have the same hang-ups about sharing his emotions as Adam did.

At the door of Frankie's room, he turned to glance back at her. "By the way, good catch on those wheezes earlier. You helped save that little girl's life."

"Thanks." She blushed, surprised by his compliment. Before she could say anything more, he flashed that amazing smile and left.

Luis was a great guy. A few months ago, she would have been thrilled to go out with him. Then again, a few months ago she hadn't been nearly as self-confident—in her nursing abilities or on a personal level.

But not anymore. For the first time in months, she didn't feel as if she were sitting in Danielle's shadow. She was a competent pediatric nurse and an attractive woman.

Too bad her heart was set on the one man who didn't want her in the same way she wanted him.

***

ADAM COULDN'T PRY Krista out of his mind. After he'd gone home the previous night, he'd thought about her until he'd fallen asleep. And she was the first person that popped into his mind when he woke up the following morning.

He needed to talk to her. Soon. Today. He needed to tell her about the accident and about losing his son. She deserved the truth.

And maybe he needed her absolution.

There wasn't time to drive past Nancy Williamson's house before work. He had early patients scheduled that morning. When he walked into the clinic, he heard the Christmas song *Winter Wonderland* and immediately thought of Krista. He could still see her so clearly in his mind, holding Joy and humming along as the carolers sang.

At this rate he'd never get her out of his head.

The clinic schedule was packed for the morning, but surprisingly light in the afternoon. Maybe because tomorrow was Christmas Eve, and most people were only coming in if their child was really sick. As he took a quick break from lunch, his mother called, demanding to know if he invited Krista to the annual Monroe holiday gathering on Christmas Day.

"I'm sorry she can't come, she's working."

"Working?" His mother's disappointment radiated over the line. "Can't she take off?"

"On Christmas Day? Someone has to work the holiday," he said in a gentle tone. He'd done his fair share of holidays as had Amber and Andrea. "I'm sure all the nurses would love to have the day off. I'll ask her again, just in case she's really not needed."

"Alright." His mother sighed. "See you on Wednesday.

"I'll be there," he promised, before ending the call.

He stared in the distance for a moment. His mother wasn't the only one disappointed to know Krista had to work the holiday.

He wanted to share Christmas with her, too.

He wasn't sure how it had happened, but somehow Krista made him forget the sadness of the holiday. It had been years since he'd had fun playing in the snow. And just the memory of her in that red strapless gown made his mouth go dry. Shaking off the memories, he stood and prepared to see his next patient. Two more to go before he could head to the hospital to make rounds.

He hadn't heard anything about Joy's mother. Alec had promised to go over there sometime this morning, since he couldn't. He suspected Nancy Williamson wasn't living in the tiny bungalow anymore. But where was she? Had she moved in with a friend? Or worse was she on the street? He hoped and prayed she'd found refuge in a shelter.

Regardless of where she was living, he'd have to discharge Joy this afternoon. He was only holding off because he still hoped Nancy would show. And that they'd have some answers as to why she'd given up her baby girl.

His next patient was a tall, gangly, adolescent girl who was complaining of a sore throat. Her throat looked red and inflamed, but he didn't know for sure if the cause was strep or mononucleosis. He suspected the latter but hoped for the former.

"I have to run a few tests," he told Erica's mother. "If it's strep we can give her antibiotics and she'll be better in a few days. If she has mono, there isn't much we can do other than treat her symptoms."

"Oh no." Erica's mother looked concerned. "If she has mono, do we have to cancel our Christmas plans?"

"Let's wait and see what she has," Adam hedged. Mononucleosis was very infectious, but he didn't want to borrow trouble. While he waited for the rapid strep and mono tests to be done, he saw his last patient and ordered more antibiotics. Some days it seemed as if he was running a special on them.

Doris poked her head around the corner. "The lab results for Erica Jones are finished. She's positive for mono."

That's what he'd thought. "Thanks Doris." He turned and headed into the room.

"I'm afraid Erica does have mono," he informed them. "I hate to ruin your holiday, but she really shouldn't have contact with other kids right now. At least not for the next week or so."

"Oh, Erica." Her mother gave her a quick hug. "I'm so sorry."

The teenager's expression was glum. "That's okay, Mom. You can go to Grandma and Grandpa's house without me. I don't want to wreck your Christmas."

"Don't be silly. We love you. We're not going without you," her mother chided. "We'll get together another time, maybe for the New Year when you're feeling better."

"Good idea." He smiled. "Make sure you get lots of rest."

"I could sleep all day," Erica admitted.

He thought about what Erica had said about not wanting to wreck Christmas. He'd been doing the same thing, avoiding telling Krista the upsetting details about the accident, especially his role in it, because he didn't want to wreck her faith in him.

That wasn't fair. He had to believe she'd be there for him, no matter what.

The hour was almost three o'clock in the afternoon. Perfect timing, as he wanted to check on Joy and hopefully run into Krista at the same time. At least, he was assuming she was working the evening shift again today.

Maybe they could grab a quick break together and talk. Now that he'd made-up his mind to tell her the truth, he was impatient to see her.

It was brutally cold outside, and the only bright spot in the subzero temperatures was that it was too cold to snow. He pulled up the collar of his coat as he walked from the parking lot to the hospital.

On the sixth floor, he went down the south wing and headed straight to Joy's room. He stopped inside the doorway when he caught a glimpse of Krista rocking Joy to sleep.

His heart squeezed in his chest. She looked so beautiful. The perfect mother for his children.

Whoa, wait a minute. His children? Since losing his son, he hadn't been able the bear the thought of having more children.

The tension around his heart eased. Somehow it was easier to imagine a future with Krista at his side. If she would forgive him.

He cleared his throat and knocked on the door. "Hi, Krista."

"Hi." She stopped rocking, looking flustered. "Are you here alone?" She peered past him, as the expecting to see someone standing beside him. Like Joy's mother. "Do you need to examine Joy?"

"Yes." He didn't think he could avoid discharging the baby any longer. There was just enough time to talk to Shirley to see what his options were. Maybe the state wouldn't mind if he waited until after Christmas. He stepped into the room. "How are you?"

"Me?" She carried Joy to the crib. "I'm fine."

She looked upset, but before he could say anything more, his cell rang. He recognized Alec's number. Finally. He answered the call. "Alec? Have you found her yet?"

"Adam, this is Amber. I'm using Alec's phone." His sister sounded upset, her nose stuffy as if she'd been crying. "We're here at Trinity Medical Center with Jillian. She's bleeding, Adam." Amber's voice hitched. "It's possible she's losing the baby."

CHAPTER THIRTEEN

Krista knew something was wrong when Adam's face paled, his expression turning as hard as granite.

He didn't so much as glance at her. "I'll be right there." He lowered the phone and strode quickly toward the door.

"Adam, wait." She caught the sleeve of his leather jacket. "What is it? What's wrong?"

"Jillian might be losing the baby." His terse voice cut deep. "I have to go."

"I'll come with you." She didn't hesitate to make the offer because she'd switched to work the day shift due to a sick call. She had only lingered to spend more time with Joy. "It will only take a minute for me to grab my purse and my coat from the locker room. "

"No." Adam's curt tone stopped her, especially when he pulled out of her grasp. "There's no need for you to be there. It's better if I go alone."

Better to go alone? For whom? Stunned, she stared at him as he strode out of Joy's room without looking back.

His abrupt dismissal hurt. More than she'd ever thought possible. What was going on with him, anyway? Once again, he had emotionally withdrawn from her, shutting her out of his life during a time of crisis.

Did she need any more proof that he wasn't interested in a long-term relationship? Seemed as if he'd made his intentions crystal clear.

Feeling sick at heart, she sank into the rocking chair.

Adam didn't need her. And he certainly didn't love her.

Not the way she loved and needed him.

ADAM STRODE down the hall of Trinity Medical Center to the waiting area on the seventh floor where the labor and delivery unit was located.

He wasn't surprised to see most of his family had already gathered there. His parents were seated next to each other, his father's strong arm hooked around his mother's slim shoulders. Amber and Nick were there, along with Andrea and her husband Stuart. Shannon sat next to Bethany and Ben, Andrea and Stewart's two kids. Even Austin was there, looking grim as usual.

The mood in the room was understandably somber. His mother's eyes looked suspiciously bright, as if she had been crying. Even the kids were unnaturally quiet. Taking up a position at the back of the room, his back pressed against the wall, he was glad he hadn't taken Krista up on her offer to skip work to come with him. The situation here with his family was awkward enough.

He knew, more than anyone, just how helpless Alec was feeling right now.

"Have you heard anything yet?" He asked, breaking the silence.

"No." Amber lifted her head from her husband's chest,

lines of concern bracketing her mouth. He understood this was probably hitting her hard, since she was pregnant as well. "Alec said he'd let us know when he has news."

"A little spotting doesn't necessarily mean the pregnancy is in trouble," his mother said in a soft tone. "I had spotting with my second pregnancy, too, and Andrea is proof that everything worked out in the long run."

"I didn't know that," Andrea said. Adam figured his mother was trying to remain positive for Shannon's sake. "I will be more than happy to find out we've all been sitting here worrying over nothing."

He would, too. But didn't believe it. The nauseous feeling in his stomach reminded him too much of the past. Glancing at Amber and Nick, he could see his younger sister didn't believe it either.

Time seemed to stand still. Or maybe it just moved with excruciating slowness. Every time he glanced at the clock, it was barely a minute since the last time he checked.

After what seemed like forever, Alec walked in, his shoulders slumped and his expression grim. He went straight over to Shannon and pulled her into his arms for a big hug.

"I'm sorry, Jillian lost the baby," he said in a choked voice.

"No!" Shannon cried, burying her face against Alec's chest, her little shoulders shaking with sobs.

"Shh, it's alright," Alec soothed, maintaining a brave front, although Adam could tell his brother was close to losing it. "The doctor says there's a reason this happened. The baby wasn't strong enough to survive. Jillian is fine. The doctor said we can try again in a few months." He smoothed the hand down Shannon's hair. "Don't cry. We're going to be okay. Our baby is in heaven with God."

Adam tore his gaze away, unable to bear his brother's pain. The situation with Jillian was very different from what he'd experienced. She'd only been nine weeks pregnant, not eighteen as Danielle had been.

And more importantly, Jillian hadn't lost her baby as a result of a man's carelessness.

"Are they going to discharge Jillian?" Amber asked, her eyes damp with tears.

Alec shook his head. "Not yet. They want to keep an eye on her for a while." He glanced at his daughter. "Shannon, honey, do you mind staying overnight with Aunt Andrea and Bethany?"

The little girl sniffled and swiped at her eyes. Bravely, she shook her head. "No, I don't mind, Daddy. If that's what you think is best."

Alec sent a questioning glance at Andrea, who hastened to reassure him. "It's no problem having Shannon stay with us. You know she's always welcome."

"Thanks." Fatigue and sorrow etched deep grooves in Alec's face. "I'd like to stay here with Jillian."

Adam pushed away from the wall stepping further into the room. "Alec, I know how you feel. Losing a baby, even one that hasn't been born yet, is difficult. I want you to know the loss will get easier over time. At least it did for me."

The varying shocked expressions on his family's faces made him realize what he just said. For the first time in a year, he'd mentioned his son.

"You lost a baby Adam?" Amber pulled away from her husband, eyeing him curiously. "Who was pregnant?"

"Danielle." He shoved his hands into his pockets, debating telling them the rest. But he couldn't quite bring himself to explain how it had been all his fault. "I'm sorry Mom and Dad. Danielle was eighteen weeks pregnant when we were in a car accident last year, right before Christmas. Our son was stillborn." He glanced at his father. "The hospital chaplain baptized him. I named him after you. Abraham Joseph Monroe."

"Oh, Adam. Why didn't you tell us?" his mother asked. "We would have been there for you."

"Danielle didn't want anyone to know." As he looked and his family, he realized how much heed needed their support back then. And now. It was unfair of Danielle to ask him to keep it quiet. The way his family surrounded Alec and Jillian had driven the point home. "Not all her fault, though," he added. "I couldn't talk about it either." Overwhelming guilt had kept the secret festering in his heart. "I'm sorry I didn't tell you sooner."

"You don't have to apologize to us," Alec said, giving Shannon one last hug before rising to his feet. "But you know we would have been there for you no matter what."

Adam nodded but couldn't speak.

"I need to get back to Jillian, but thanks for telling us." Alec looked thoughtful. "You've made me feel better that Jillian and I have each other to get through this, which is more than you had."

That much was true. He knew Alec and Jillian's love would draw them closer during this time of crisis. They'd support each other, which would only help to ease the pain.

The opposite of what he and Danielle had experienced. Their relationship had been on the rocks and losing their son had been the final straw.

Alec's gaze shifted to something behind him. He turned in time to see Krista standing in the doorway of the waiting room, her gaze stricken.

She'd heard every word.

He inwardly winced. This was not good. He should have told her first.

"Krista," he began, moving to cross over to her. She spun on her heel and hurried away from him.

Straight toward the elevator at the end of the hall.

FIGHTING TEARS, Krista quickened her pace, anxious to get far away from Adam.

He'd never told her Danielle had been pregnant. Hadn't told her about losing his son. Or even mentioned his son's name. Not once in the time they'd spent together.

What else had he kept from her?

"Krista." She heard Adam behind her but didn't trust herself to turn around. She was afraid she'd end up settling for whatever scraps he'd chosen to give her.

She deserved better. Her head knew that much, although her heart felt as if it had been ripped from her chest and shredded into tiny bits.

When she reached the elevator, the doors opened, allowing several people to step out. She slipped past them then quickly pressed the button to go down. When the elevator didn't move fast enough, she stabbed the button to close the doors even as Adam called her name again.

He wasn't quick enough. The doors closed and the elevator began to slide downward. Alone, she sagged against the wall, burying her face in her hands, her eyes burning with tears.

She couldn't face him. Not now and maybe not ever. Well, she couldn't avoid Adam forever, as she was a pediatric nurse and would likely end up caring for his patients.

But she still needed time to marshal her defenses against him.

Time to convince herself the wisest choice would be to get over him, once and for all.

SHE DIDN'T GO STRAIGHT HOME. STARING at the four walls in her empty apartment didn't hold much appeal. Instead, she headed to the mall, losing herself among the harried Christmas shoppers.

She wandered from one store to the next, not seeing anything, her stomach knotted to the point of acute pain. She thought it had been difficult before, when she'd had a crush on Adam while he'd belonged to Danielle. This feeling of loss was much, much worse.

Because she loved him. Loved him with her entire heart and soul. And wanted the same in return.

He kept so much of his personal life hidden away from her. Had Danielle felt the same way? Had Adam refused to share every aspect of his life with her sister? Was that why they had broken up? It was still difficult to grasp that her sister had miscarried a baby and never told her. Had Adam pulled away from her then, as well? Was his lack of emotion part of what had broken them up after the miscarriage?

Her head ached with the effort of holding back tears. She really needed to get a grip on her emotions. Feeling this level of acute devastation wasn't healthy.

She stood in front of a bright Christmas display without seeing the flash of lights, or the colorful ornaments on the tree. All she could think about was how glad she was that to be scheduled to work the holiday. Maybe she could work a double shift. Sitting home alone would have been so much worse.

Lost in her misery, she didn't realize how many hours had passed until the mall shops began to close. With a start, she glanced at her watch, realizing it was nine o'clock at night.

She trudged to her car, dreading the idea of going home when she needed someone to talk to. Not that she had another option. Flying to London to be with her sister wasn't possible when she was committed to work over the next few days.

Could she call her sister? London was six hours ahead. If she called Danielle now it would be the middle of the night.

No, she'd have to wait until the morning. Danielle was a night owl, but not even her sister stayed up on a routine basis until the wee hours of the morning.

Mr. Baumgartner was sprinkling sand on the sidewalks when she arrived at her apartment.

"Hello, Mr. Baumgartner," she greeted him as she approached.

The older man looked up at her. "The Olsons have given their notice, they're moving out of their two-bedroom apartment on February 1st. Are you still interested in upgrading your place?"

She paused, realizing there was no need now that Joy's mother had likely been found. Although there had been no sign of the woman yet. She nodded. She still intended to become a foster mother. If not for Joy, then for the next small baby who needed her. She'd have a family, one way or another. "Yes," she said. "I'm very interested."

"Fine, I'll slot you in." Mr. Baumgartner shook another handful of sand on the sidewalk. "If you change your mind for some reason, let me know. I won't advertise until after the first of the year anyway."

"Thanks. I won't change my mind." She walked past him, using her key to let her into the apartment building.

Instead of trying to get some sleep, she sat for hours, doing the math and figuring out ways to financially swing the more expensive two-bedroom apartment the Olsens would be vacating.

The idea of being a foster mother helped ease her despair. She wanted to help take care of children in need. Kids like her and Danielle, who desperately needed a family. And taking control of her life felt good. Or at least dulled the pain of losing Adam.

Losing him wasn't exactly the right phrase. Obviously she'd never had him in the first place.

She stared at her notes. One extra overtime shift at pay period would carry her through the next few months until she had her credit card bill paid off. After that she'd be in the clear. If she worked hard enough and watched her expenses, she could make the two bedroom apartment work.

Unlike Adam's feelings toward her, which she could not change, no matter how much she wished she could. The way he closed himself off from others, especially from her, was something he needed to change on his own.

If he wanted to.

THE NEXT MORNING Krista dragged herself out of bed with a groan, rubbing her gritty, red rimmed eyes. She hadn't slept much but needed to get ready for work. Besides, she wanted to go in early to spend time with Joy. If the baby was still there. She'd felt certain Adam had intended to discharge the baby yesterday.

And she also needed to bring the Christmas gifts she'd purchased for the unit.

Her cell phone rang and she tensed, wondering if the caller was Adam. A glance at the screen though proved it wasn't. "Hello?"

"Krista?" Danielle's husky voice flowed over the line. "How are you?"

"Great." She forced cheerfulness into her tone. "I'm glad you called. I was thinking of you last night." The baby her sister and Adam had lost had weighed heavily on her mind, but today she decided there was no reason to bring it up. Adam was still upset over the loss, whereas Danielle had moved on.

"I've been thinking about you, too." Danielle's bubbly tone was infectious. "How do you feel about taking a trip out here to see me?"

This was the first time Danielle had offered to have Krista come and visit. Surprised and pleased, she answered, "Wow, I would love to, but I don't think I can swing it financially. Maybe some day, though. I miss you, Danielle. I'd love to see you again."

"I miss you, too." A deep voice murmured in the background. Her sister obviously wasn't alone. "Listen, Mario wants you to know he'll help foot the bill for your trip here. In fact, he's the reason I called. Mario has asked me to marry him and I've accepted."

"Danielle! I'm so happy for you." And she truly was thrilled for her sister. Danielle deserved to find love.

"Thanks, Krista. The wedding isn't going to be until next summer, and I was really hoping you'd stand up as my maid of honor."

"Of course I'll stand up for you," she agreed without hesitation. Summer was months away. If she finagled her finances, she might be able to swing it. Especially if Mario helped. She could always work more extra shifts. And who knew how long it would take for her to get assigned a foster baby? "I wouldn't miss your wedding for anything, Danielle. Count me in."

"Wonderful. I'll let you know a date as soon as we've picked one." Danielle laughed. "I am so happy, Krista. This move was the best thing that's ever happened to me."

"I'm glad." She was truly thrilled for Danielle.

"What about you? How are things going?" Her sister sounded interested.

"They're great." She didn't want to dampen Danielle's enthusiasm by bringing up the problems of her love life, yet she needed to at least let Danielle know about Adam. "I love my job at Children's Memorial."

"Children's Memorial?" Danielle sounded surprised. "Have you run into Adam?"

That was one way to put it. "Yes, I have. I've taken care of a few of his patients."

"How is he?" Danielle asked. "I hope he's found happiness the way I have."

He hadn't but she refrained from saying anything more. "He seems fine. He's a great doctor."

"I'm sure he's a good doctor and a wonderful guy," Danielle agreed. "If you see him, let him know I wish him well. He and I weren't good together, he was far too intense for me. And we didn't really see eye to eye on a lot of things. But I don't hold any hard feelings against him."

Intense? Odd that Danielle saw him as intense when she'd only glimpsed his aloofness. Had losing his son changed him that much?

"I will." She had no plan to talk to Adam anytime soon. Except when it came to caring for his patients. "Take care of yourself, Danielle. Give Mario a hug for me and send me some pictures if you have them."

"I have pictures. I'll text them to you now. Bye, Krista. Merry Christmas!"

"Merry Christmas, Danielle." She disconnected from the call, considering her sister's comments.

She had to admit the Adam she'd known a year ago was different from the man she knew now. He had changed after losing his son. How could he not? For years she'd thought of him as the perfect man, kind, considerate, always there when she needed him.

No one was perfect. She knew that. Yet she'd still gotten upset with him because he'd emotionally withdrawn after losing his son.

A loss she could barely comprehend.

Maybe she was being unfair. Yet he was the one who had kept the miscarriage a secret from her. A quick glance at the clock confirmed she needed to get moving, if she wanted to spend time with Joy. Would she see Adam? If so she'd better figure out what she was going to say after running off on him yesterday.

Some of her anger and resentment had faded. She was disappointed and hurt at the way he'd consistently pulled away from her, but it was difficult to remain angry. He'd kept his secrets not just from her, but from his family.

Why? Out of some sort of misplaced guilt?

At Children's Memorial, the staff parking lot was nearly empty. Only the hospital staff who had to work the holiday showed up on Christmas Eve.

She parked and then lifted the huge bag of gifts from the back seat of her car. On the sixth floor, she stopped in the staff locker room to hang up her coat and lock up her purse. She dropped the bag of gifts in the nurses' station, then headed straight to Joy's room.

She halted in the doorway when she saw a strange woman sitting in a rocking chair, holding Joy.

The woman's gaze was riveted on the baby, staring down at her with an expression of utter rapture. Oddly, she hadn't glanced up when Krista entered the room.

She must be Joy's mother.

CHAPTER FOURTEEN

Krista wasn't sure what to do—staying seemed an invasion of privacy but she couldn't simply leave, not without at least talking to Joy's mother. As if her feet had a will of their own, they carried her further into the room.

The woman cradled Joy in her arms and the love shining from her eyes eased the concern tightening her stomach. Before she could introduce herself, Adam came into the room.

"There you are, Krista, I've been looking for you." He abruptly paused when he saw Joy's mother holding the baby. "Nancy?" He took another step toward the woman. "Are you Nancy Williamson?"

The woman went still, staring at them with wide, frightened gaze. She looked between her and Adam as of trying to figure out what they wanted.

"Are you Nancy Williamson?" Adam asked again.

Slowly the woman nodded.

"You're Joy's mother? You left her in my clinic, but now you've come back to claim her?" Adam persisted.

A shadow of uncertainty darkened the woman's gaze. Krista could tell she didn't understand what Adam had said.

Suddenly the puzzle pieces slipped into place. She probably should have realized sooner. Stepping forward, she mouthed the word mother and used her right hand to spell out the word in sign language.

Nancy looked relieved and nodded again. She raised a hand and made several sign language gestures that Krista didn't understand.

"I don't believe it." Adam glanced at Krista in amazement. "Joy's mother is deaf, too? How did you figure it out?"

"I could tell she didn't understand. I think you spoke too fast for her to read your lips." She turned back to Nancy, realizing this additional news clarified things. "It makes sense now why she felt she couldn't take care of a baby all alone," she murmured. "I'm sure it's been very difficult, caring for a child when you can't hear the baby crying. She may not have any help, maybe she's been caring for Joy all by herself."

"Good point." Adam blew out a breath. "We need to get Shirley in here as soon as possible. Before she leaves for the day."

"I agree." she moved closer to Nancy and Joy. Using the only sign language she knew, the alphabet, Krista asked if Nancy knew her baby was also deaf.

The shocked expression on Nancy's features confirmed she hadn't known. It must not have occurred to Nancy to have Joy tested, maybe because the baby was so young. Nancy slowly shook her head, closed her eyes, and held Joy close.

"She didn't know about Joy's deafness," Adam said in a low tone. "No wonder she didn't turn around when I spoke to her that first day."

"You spoke to her?" That was a surprise.

"I saw her outside my clinic and suspected she was Joy's mother. When I called out to her though, she ignored me and hurried away."

Nancy stood and carefully set Joy in the crib. Then she pulled a small notebook and stubby pencil from her pocket and began to write. Krista exchanged a glance with Adam as they waited for her to finish. She ripped the page out of the notebook and handed it to Adam.

He read it out loud. "The note you left in my door gave me hope. I came here to the hospital and found Joy. But being a deaf woman raising a child who could hear seemed unfair. I couldn't talk to my child and sometimes I would see her crying and wondered how long she'd been upset. I didn't know how I was going to cope. I missed a few house payments and the bank is about to foreclose on my loan. I love Joy, but I was scared. I wanted a better life for her than she'd have with me."

Krista blinked back tears.

Adam turned the note over and wrote back. Krista stepped closer to read over his shoulder. "I will help you. There are plenty of resources available. There are ways to help you learn to take care of a baby, systems that can be used to alert you to her crying. You are not alone in this."

Nancy took the note and her expression turned hopeful when she read what Adam had written. Then she wrote again, ripping the note off and handing it to Adam. "Am I too late? Does Joy belong to someone else?"

Krista shook her head. "No, you are not too late." She spoke slowly emphasizing each word then she used sign language to spell the word yours. She picked Joy up and placed the baby back into Nancy's arms, demonstrating what she meant. "Yours," she repeated. "Joy is your daughter."

Nancy's eyes filled with gratitude. "Thank you." She mouthed. Nancy lifted her fingers to her lips and drew them away, making the sign for thank you.

"You're very welcome." Krista would miss the baby but could rest easy knowing Joy would be well cared for with a mother who loved her very much.

She couldn't ask for anything more than that.

ADAM HAD WANTED a few moments alone with Krista, but Nancy's arrival had caused a flurry activity. There were forms to fill out, arrangements to be made before he could legally discharge Joy into Nancy's care. He was willing to make her payments himself to help get her back on her feet financially. Seeing as it was Christmas Eve, he couldn't imagine a better Christmas gift than reuniting a woman and her daughter.

Krista disappeared shortly after Shirley had arrived, saying something about needing to get to work. At first he was worried she was upset, but when she gave Nancy a hug, he realized she wasn't. She'd claimed she wanted the best for Joy and she'd meant it. As usual, Krista was being her normal, generous self.

He knew he'd messed up, badly. Last night, after leaving Alec and Jillian at the hospital, he'd gone back to Children's Memorial, only to discover Krista wasn't there. He'd been surprised to learn she'd worked the day shift to cover a sick call. He'd wrongly assumed she'd left work to find him at Trinity Medical Center.

He wished he could go back and do things differently.

Like telling her the truth first, before blurting out the details to his family. To explain why he kept the secret in the first place.

He'd tried her apartment, but she wasn't there either. The windows were dark and there was no sign of her car in the parking lot. It didn't take a genius to figure out she wasn't home. He tried calling, but her phone had gone to voicemail as if she'd turned it off. He hadn't bothered to leave a message.

Better that he apologize in person.

It took him several hours to get everything arranged for Joy and Nancy. He'd interviewed Nancy with the sign language interpreter nearby, to make sure there were no drug or alcohol related issues. By the time he'd finished, he was convinced that Nancy's deafness and getting behind on her mortgage were the reasons she'd given up the baby. In talking the situation over with Shirley, they'd agreed to keep Joy in the hospital until the day after Christmas. He needed time to work with the bank, and to arrange the resources the mother and daughter would need moving forward. Nancy could spend the nights in Joy's room with her until then.

If only it was as easy to fix things with Krista. She had to work until eleven-thirty that night, giving him little choice but to wait for her to get off before they could talk.

He spent some time at his parents' house, helping to get food ready for the Monroe family celebration. He'd asked his family to move their gathering up to an earlier time on Christmas Day, knowing Krista would be off work in the morning and therefore able to attend.

If he could convince her to give him another chance.

He finished his Christmas shopping, spending a solid hour picking out the proper gift for Krista. By eleven o'clock that night, he couldn't stand waiting another minute. Even though he knew she still had a half hour left on her shift, he drove to Children's Memorial, his Christmas gift wrapped and sitting on the seat beside him.

Tucking the small gift wrapped box in his pocket, he made his way to the sixth floor. When he saw Krista walking off the unit with a small group of nurses, he realized he'd almost missed her. They must have gotten out earlier than usual.

"Krista? Do you have a minute?"

She didn't smile but paused and slowly nodded. "Sure."

He waited until the rest of the nursing staff had left them alone. Taking her arm in his hand, he steered her toward the small waiting area outside the unit. Thankfully it was empty. The Christmas tree in the corner gave the room a festive look.

How should he start? He took a deep breath and let it out slowly. "I'm sorry, Krista. You shouldn't have found out about how I lost my son the way you did. I should have told you the truth myself."

She didn't seem angry but regarded him thoughtfully. "Why didn't you?"

He was silent for a long moment. There were lots of reasons, but there was really only one that mattered. "Because his death was my fault."

"Your fault?" She frowned. "Danielle's miscarriage was your fault?"

"Yes. I was arguing with her that night, while driving. We argued a lot back in those days." That was an understatement. "I didn't see the truck coming straight at us until it was too late."

"Oh, Adam." She reached for his hand. He fought the urge to pull her closer, to lose himself in her embrace.

"Danielle told me the accident was caused by a truck running a red light. That's not your fault."

"It was my fault." He stared down at their clasped hands. "There was time to avoid the crash. I tried to veer out of the way. But it was too late."

After a pause she said, "I don't agree. Would it have been your fault if you were laughing over some silly joke, instead of arguing?"

Her question caught him off guard. If he and Danielle had been laughing, having fun before the crash, would he still be plagued by guilt? "I don't know. Maybe. I should have been paying attention."

"That truck ran a red light. That's not easy to anticipate even if you are paying attention. I don't blame you for your son's death." Her smile was sad. "It is not up to us to question God's plan. Not to mention, Jesus forgives our sins. I think you need to find a way to forgive yourself."

"I'm trying," he admitted. "Because of you."

She blinked. "Me?"

"Yes. Losing Abe was bad enough but losing you would be so much worse. When you ditched me at the hospital last night, I nearly went crazy looking for you." He pulled the small, gift-wrapped box out of his pocket and handed it to her. "Will you please open this?"

She hesitated so long he thought she was going to refuse. Then she took the box and slowly unwrapped it. Her eyes widened when she saw the jeweler's box, and she flipped little the lid open, her gaze full of hope mixed with trepidation.

She stared at the ring. What was wrong? Did she hate diamonds? He should have asked, rather than assuming. Danielle had wanted to pick out her own engagement ring.

He should have anticipated Krista would want to do the same.

"If you don't like it, we can exchange it for something else." His words sounded stiff and awkward to his own ears.

"I don't understand." Her gaze held confusion. "Why are you giving this to me?"

What was not to understand? He frowned. "Because I love you."

"You love me?" He couldn't tell if she was happy or sad. "I want to believe you, Adam. But every time you're hurt or upset, you close yourself off from me. I have to be honest—that isn't exactly the foundation of a loving relationship."

He swallowed hard, panic threatening to choke him. "I know I've held myself back from you, and I'm sorry. I can't prove it, but I was planning to talk to you the day I found out about Alec and Jillian. I've had so many regrets but turning around to see you standing with that devastated expression on your face was the worst." He tightened his grip on her hand. "I'm sorry I hurt you. You're a beautiful, kind, generous person. Will you please give me another chance to prove how much I love you?"

A slow smile broke across her features, and she nodded. "Yes, Adam. Because I love you, too." He couldn't hide his elation, even when she held up a hand and added, "But I want you to share everything with me. I want you to tell me what you're thinking and feeling, even if you're afraid it might upset me."

It sounded easy, but he knew it wasn't. His happiness faded and his gaze turned serious. "I will try, Krista. I swear to you I will try." And he would do his best, but hiding his emotions deep inside had become an ingrained habit, especially over this past year. He needed to be honest with her.

"Old patterns can be hard to break. I need you to know I might slip up on occasion."

"At least you're being honest." She read his thoughts easier than Danielle ever had. "I understand you've hidden your emotions for a long time. I don't expect perfection, I just need to know you care."

"I do care, more than I can ever say". He reached out and drew her close. "I love you, Krista. I can't imagine my life without you."

"Oh, Adam." She wrapped her arms around his neck, holding him tight. "I love you. I think I've always loved you since the night you came to rescue me from that terrible date." She gazed up at him from dark eyes bright with tears. "I just didn't want to settle for being second best. Or for anything less than having your love."

"You could never be second best." He gently took the box from her hand, opened it and took out the diamond engagement ring. "And you will always have my love. Will you wear my ring? Will you marry me?"

"Yes. I will marry you, Adam."

He slipped the ring on her finger with a sense of relief. "Thank heavens. My mother was ready to disown me for hurting you. And I was afraid Austin was going to ask you to marry him, just to make me mad."

That made her laugh. "He wouldn't do that."

"Yes, he would, because he knows a good thing when he sees it." He arched a brow. "I hope you know what you're getting into now that you've agreed to become a part of the Monroe family. My parents are going to expect a lot of grandchildren. I think I'd like to oblige them."

"I'm not worried." She smiled. I'll love being a part of your family." She stood on tiptoe to kiss him.

He met her halfway, kissing her with a need born of

desperation. Only knowing that they were still standing in the waiting room at Children's Memorial held him in check. He broke off from the kiss while he still could.

"Merry Christmas, Adam." A hint of remorse shadowed her eyes. "I don't have a present for you."

"You've already given me a gift, by forgiving me and agreeing to marry me. I love you." He drew her toward the elevator, knowing God had once again blessed the Monroe clan.

Thanks to Krista, Christmas had just become his favorite holiday.

EPILOGUE

Krista smiled as Adam's family surrounded Nancy and Joy Williamson, cooing over the baby while drawing them firmly into the living room, making them feel welcome at their Christmas family gathering.

She was so happy they'd agreed to come.

Nancy smiled and handed Joy to Krista so she could take off her coat and scarf.

She gazed into Joy's tiny face, until Nancy came back for her. As she handed Joy to her mother, she was pleased at how Joy's bright eyes widened at all the attention.

"Having regrets?" Adam murmured near her ear.

"Not a single one." During the commotion with Nancy, Shirley had briefly mentioned that Krista had been approved to be a foster mother. She was thrilled when Adam had agreed to take a part in the process too. He liked the idea of helping kids in need as much as she did. "It was nice of you to invite them. And to pick them up from the hospital to bring them here."

"It was the least I could do, considering Joy helped to

bring us together." Adam's smile warmed her all the way down to her frozen toes.

"Yes." The baby would always hold a special place in her heart for that same reason. Joy was a miracle baby.

"What can I get everyone to drink?" Abe asked beaming at the family gathered around him. "Hot cider, anyone?"

He handed a cup to Nancy who tentatively tasted it before grinning and nodding. Everyone made a point of speaking slowly and distinctly to Nancy to help ensure she could understand them.

And if not, Nancy always had her notepad handy.

Alec and Jillian seemed to be doing better, despite their recent loss. Jillian smiled and took Joy's tiny hand, her eyes revealing a hint of longing. Shannon didn't venture far from Jillian's side. She suspected that Alec and Jillian were doing their best to put the miscarriage into perspective by focusing on their beautiful daughter.

As the Monroe family gathered in the living room, near the giant, brightly decorated tree, Krista couldn't imagine being any happier than she was right at that moment.

"Can I have your attention?" Adam's deep voice was remarkably similar to his father's.

The group quieted down, looking up at him expectantly.

Adam drew her close to his side. "I'm thrilled to announce our engagement. Krista has agreed to marry me."

"Yay!" Amber jumped to her feet. "Welcome to the family, Krista."

She found herself being hugged and kissed by several members of the Monroe family. Even Austin had the audacity to kiss her on the mouth, sending her a secret wink when Adam frowned.

Nancy must have understood because she was smiling

and made a sign that Krista believed meant congratulations. She really needed to brush up on her sign language.

"Good choice, Adam." Abe clapped his son on the back. "This time your mother and I wholeheartedly approve."

This time? She glanced at Adam, her brow raised questionably. It sounded as if his parents hadn't approved of his engagement to Danielle.

Adam gave her a small nod. "I'm glad, Dad." He pulled her in for another quick kiss. "Because I think Krista is perfect for me, too.

Tears threatened and she blinked them back with an effort.

So this was how it felt to be a part of a loving family.

I HOPE you enjoyed *Holiday Haven*, the third book in my Monroe Family series. Are you ready to read Austin and Lindsey's story in *Shattered Trust*? Click Here!

DEAR READER

Thanks so much for reading my Monroe Family series. I'm truly blessed to have wonderful readers like you. I'm working on Austin and Lindsey's story now and will have that ready to go by February of next year.

Don't forget, you can purchase eBooks or audiobooks directly from my website will receive a 15% discount by using the code **LauraScott15**. I hope to have *Shattered Trust* available on my website by early January.

I adore hearing from my readers! I can be found through my website at https://www.laurascottbooks.com, via Facebook at https://www.facebook.com/LauraScott Books, Instagram at https://www.instagram.com/laurascott books/, and Twitter https://twitter.com/laurascottbooks. Please take a moment to subscribe to my YouTube channel at youtube.com/@LauraScottBooks-wr1xl?sub_confirmation=1. Also, take a moment to sign up for my monthly newsletter to learn about my new book releases! All subscribers receive a free novella not available for purchase on any platform.

Until next time,
Laura Scott
PS. Keep reading for a sneak peak of *Shattered Trust*.

SHATTERED TRUST

Prologue

"Head for the river! *Run!*"

Austin Monroe could barely hear Sam's voice over the roar of the wildfire bearing down on them. He didn't need his buddy's urging to keep him moving—the heat of the fire scorching his back was motivation enough. The wind had shifted, bringing the fire they'd been fighting straight toward them, breaking through the line. If not for Sam coming back to warn him, he would have been burned to a crisp.

They still might die.

Even as the realization sink deep, he caught sight of the river less than fifty yards ahead. Reaching the river before the fire caught up to them was their only chance of survival.

A slim chance, if the severe drought hadn't made the river too low.

The heavy Kevlar suit he wore wasn't enough to keep the force of the heat off him. He ignored the sweat rolling into his eyes beneath the helmet as he stayed focused on the river. He slipped, nearly fell, but Sam was right behind him, dragging him upright and pushing him forward. With a herculean effort, he made his way down the bank to the water, jumping in with a feeling of relief. He doused his whole body as best he could in water that was barely knee high.

It took him a minute to realize Sam hadn't joined him in the river. He glanced back to see his partner using a drip torch to light a backfire on the grassy area surrounding the riverbank to protect them from a lethal burn over.

He pulled himself back out of the water to join Sam. They didn't have much time as the wildfire bore down on them, moving with astronomical speed as it gobbled up the dry brush with a voracious hunger.

"Get into the river!" Sam shouted as he lit as many fires as he could with the drip torch. Austin had lost his equipment when the fire had changed direction, so he couldn't do much to help.

"No." He wasn't leaving his partner, the guy who'd come back for him. He would not allow Sam to face this alone. When the drip torch was empty, Sam tossed it into the smoldering grass fire. Austin grabbed his arm. "Let's go. We need to get in the water."

This time Sam didn't argue, but finally followed him back down the bank to the river. When Austin hit the water, he felt Sam fall heavily unto him from behind, pinning him down. It seemed as if his buddy had used up all his resources to keep going. Austin reached up and pulled Sam down into the water beside him.

The backfire didn't work as well as they'd hoped. Orange flames flickered dangerously close. Following Sam's lead, Austin took a big gulp of air before submerging his head in the river leaving only the very top of his helmet above the water. He sensed Sam did the same, although the smoke was so thick it was hard to see.

Over and over again, he quickly lifted his head, gasped for what little oxygen was left in the air and then ducked his head beneath the water again.

Finally the roar of the fire subsided, indicating it had burned down, the raging beast having moved on to better prey—thick brush lining the ridge to the west of them.

"Sam?" He levered himself to his hands and knees, reaching for his friend. Sam's smoke blackened face peered up at him and his heart squeezed in his chest. Hadn't Sam continued dunking his head beneath the water? "Are you all right?"

Sam gave a tiny nod, but his breathing was harsh, labored. Austin reached for his radio, wondering just how much smoke had gotten into his buddy's lungs. "Mayday, mayday. Firefighter with smoke inhalation is down in the Rock River, two miles east of the river's bend. Need medic STAT."

"Roger that. Medevac chopper on the way."

"Sam?" Panic clawed up his back as Sam began to cough, his body convulsing so hard he could barely take a breath. "Hang on, they're coming for us. Just hang on."

"Lindsey." Sam reached up and weakly grasped Austin's jacket. "Take care of her for me. Take care of Lindsey and Josh."

Sam's plea for his wife and child stabbed his heart. His gut clenched with fear. "Don't worry about Lindsey and Josh. You're going to make it out of here to care for them yourself."

"Too late," Sam whispered between coughing fits. "Take care of them—promise me. They'll need... Promise me..." His voice faded as another coughing fit seized him.

"I promise." Austin held his partner close, scanning the smoke darkened sky. Where in the world was that chopper?

Sam stopped coughing, closed his eyes and slumped bonelessly in Austin's arms. No. No! He stared down at his buddy's face, as the medivac chopper cleared the trees and headed for them, knowing with a sick certainty that Sam was right.

It was too late.